VENGEANCE: A DARK ROMANCE

(MASTER'S PROTÉGÉ BOOK ONE)

JANE HENRY

Copyright © 2021 by Jane Henry

All rights reserved.

No part of this book may be reproduced in any form or by any electronic or mechanical means, including information storage and retrieval systems, without written permission from the author, except for the use of brief quotations in a book review.

Cover photography by Wander Aguiar

Cover design my Popkitty Designs

❦ Created with Vellum

SYNOPSIS

They call him the executioner.

Some say monster.

Dishonorably discharged from the military, he runs a highly secret, clandestine operation, and has everything I need to find the justice I crave.

Power players at his disposal.

An insatiable hunger for justice.

A reckless disregard for the law.

But when his own family becomes embroiled in a wicked play for power, he needs me as well.

I offer him my skills, but that's not what he wants.

He wants me.

And Cain Master always gets what he wants.

Please note: Vengeance is book one in the Master's Protégé duet and can not be read as a stand-alone.

CHAPTER 1

Violet

THE DRIVER PULLS OVER by the side of the road. "Here you go. Pay on the app."

I look at the GPS and note we're still a mile away. We drove by the wooden placard that read *Welcome to Salem,* complete with the obligatory golden witch on a broom, half a mile ago.

"Uh, this isn't it. Still a mile up ahead."

The kid driving the car's about twenty years old, clean-shaven, and he wears glasses perched on the end of his nose. He looks over the wire rims and frowns. "This is as far as I go, lady. Do you know who lives up that hill?"

"I do." I barely control my temper. "It was the address I gave you when you agreed to drive me, remember?"

He blinks. "I didn't recognize the address. Would've turned down the job if I had."

Lovely. Does everyone know the man I'm going to see, and I've somehow lived in ignorance all this time until yesterday?

"Soooo?"

"I won't go up there. I don't have a death wish, lady. I won't charge you for the rest of the trip, only this far," he says, as if somehow that makes it all better.

"How kind of you." I can't hide my disgust.

"Out," he snaps.

"Fine." I grab my bag, a beat up black leather crossbody I picked up at a thrift store, and sling it over my shoulder. I really should maybe find something a bit nicer for times such as these. "Thanks."

I slam the door harder than I need to and frown at my choice of footwear. I have exactly *one pair* of heels in my closet, and it figures today's the day I'd decide to wear them. I could call for another ride but that risks another rejection, and the truth is, I don't have time. I've got to be at work in two hours, and I have no idea how long this—interview?—will take.

So, I do what I must. I take a deep breath and begin walking toward the house.

I fume the whole way. If Mr. Master's asshole employee hadn't totaled my car, I wouldn't be walking alone to the ridiculously huge mansion a mile away on the hill. I wouldn't have this massive headache or bruises either.

I also never would've discovered Cain Master or have an excuse to visit him.

The summer heat's cooler by the seaside, yet it's still nearly eighty degrees with no breeze. I'll show up sweaty and disheveled, no matter how slowly or carefully I walk.

My head hurts from the injuries of the night before, but I'm otherwise alright. I used a little bit of makeup to cover the bruises, and even ran a mascara brush through my lashes. But the makeup was old and dried up, and I'm afraid I look like a little kid playing with her mom's lipstick.

Normally, I prefer to mask my eyes—they're a vivid violet that unfortunately is hard to hide—but today I decided it couldn't hurt to accent them a little. Or... whatever. I don't know what else people who know about these things would call it. Shades of purple make my eyes stand out.

The dress I chose is one of the few I own. A pale lavender number in a cotton blend, it dips in the front while still being professional, the hem hitting mid-thigh. Combined with a nude pair of pumps, the dress is professional and simple, suitable for a job like today.

It's odd that while I was able to find out Cain Master's history, including the cases brought and accusations made against him, I wasn't able to find a birth date or a single picture anywhere. It's disconcerting, honestly.

Cain Master is insignificant in the eyes of the American public... but it's a lie.

A part of me wonders if hiding damn near everything about him online was intentional. Or did he have an identity before this one? Another name? Is this one given to him by the government, or one he chose for anonymity?

I bet he isn't as quick as he once was, his wits dulled over the years. He's wealthy enough, that I know from just a cursory glance at his home. But does he even own that? I spent my time researching his history and background and haven't looked into his personal assets.

I'll get there.

He has no family to speak of, not even so much as an ex-wife.

I know enough. Sometimes it's better not to know more than what's directly in front of you.

I twist my foot on a rock and stumble but throw my arms out wide and catch myself before I fall. If I hurt myself now, I'll have to head home and cancel this mission altogether.

I carefully take off my heels and begin to walk along the side of the road. It's cooler here, under the shadows of the large, stately maples that offer shade and shelter. I'm physically fit, but panting from the heat. I blame last night's accident.

The call of a seagull over the water catches my attention. Even from here, I can see the blue-green depths of the ocean bordering his house. What would it be like to live in a place like this? I'd hazard a guess the view isn't the only reason he lives here, though.

His house is far enough off the beaten path to deter strangers from visiting—at least, most of them. No little girls in uniforms would make this walk to peddle their Girl Scout cookies, no Jehovah's Witnesses would come knocking to save his besmirched soul. It's almost a fortress of sorts, set far from the main roads, but not so far that a twenty-minute ride wouldn't bring you into the city to get food or gas.

The closest Air Force base is in Hanscom, only thirty-two minutes by car. I checked.

Here, in the light of day, when I'm not compromised and as badly injured as I was when I first arrived last night, I note things I didn't see before—a large, sunny porch that overlooks the private beach, immaculately well-kept and homey, and a pathway lined with brilliant white rocks that leads to the front door. It's like a trail to the gingerbread house, set just far enough back to beckon unsuspecting victims.

I always did have an overactive imagination.

The last time I came here, he wasn't home, and I was injured. I missed lots of details.

Here in Salem and the surrounding cities, it's unusual for a home this close to the water to be much bigger than three or four bedrooms. Small colonial homes are the bedrock of the North Shore. Much larger homes are rare and cost a small fortune.

As I draw nearer, I note a four-car garage, a large, paved, circular driveway, and two main entrances, both bedecked with large but simple wreaths. The landscaping's immaculate, well-groomed and maintained, and if I peek a bit to the right of the main entrance, I can see into a rock-lined garden that overlooks the sea. Is that a barn or a shed out back? I also catch glimpses of a heavy gate and fence and another glimmer of water. A pool?

The owner of this home favors privacy.

A brisk wind kicks up as I near the main entrance. Here, right by the water, the temperature's dropped by at least ten degrees.

I'm not alone. There's someone in the side yard tending the garden, humming as they pull weeds. A small pile of drying dandelions sits beside him. Someone else is rummaging around in the garage. I'm guessing the people I met last night aren't the only staff he employs.

At least I should be able to get someone's attention.

I walk up to the closest entrance, draw in a deep breath, and square my shoulders. The front entryway's swept neatly, and a large potted plant stands to the right. Everything's masculine and utilitarian, no welcome mat by the door, nothing flowery or bright. I ring the doorbell.

The clanging of the bell reverberates inside, a deep, musical baritone. Footsteps sound on the other side of the door, and I see a tall, thin man through the rectangular windows that flank each side of the double doors.

I let my breath out, then draw in another to steady my nerves. From here, I can see the kitchen entrance where I went in last night and the sitting room where I saw the doctor. No sign of the master of this house.

He's in there, though. I know it.

Will he see me?

When the door opens, I notice a uniformed guard standing in the shadows to the right of the doorway, armed and ready. His face is set in stone, his eyes staring at me unblinking from the shadows. Now that's a sight you don't see every day.

My pulse staggers.

I wonder if the guy at the door's a daytime butler, or housekeeper or something. He's older than I am, pale, with a receding hairline, but he's wiry and strong. When he looks at me, only one eye is seeing, the other is dull and lifeless.

He gently bows his head in greeting, and when he speaks, he has a gentle southern accent. "May I help you?"

I clear my throat. It's make-or-break time. I give him what I hope is a disarming smile, but I'm rusty with such formalities and only manage to bare my teeth at him. *Cringy.*

Step one. Confirm the name of the owner of the house. Say it with confidence.

My voice rings loud and clear. "I'm here to see Mr. Master, please."

He nods. *Check.*

"Do you have an appointment?"

I briefly consider lying just to get inside, but quickly dismiss that idea. It could backfire too quickly.

I shake my head. "I don't. Is he in?"

He holds my gaze for a moment before he responds. Is he sizing me up? He quickly schools his features and gestures for me to come in.

"I'm not sure if he is in or not, but please, have a seat and I'll find out. Your name?"

I don't believe him. He knows exactly whether or not he's in, he just doesn't want to tell me until he knows if Mr. Master's entertaining visitors.

"Violet."

"Last name as well, please, miss."

"Violet Price." The name I adopted when I turned eighteen.

He nods. "I'll be right back, Miss Price." As he walks away, he takes a phone out of his pocket and begins to type. Texting.

The guard looks at me, immovable and serious.

"Hey." I give him a little side-wave.

He doesn't even blink.

"You come here often?" Funny, Vi. Real funny. He just stares at me without responding, a real-life stoic. I sigh and turn away.

I take the opportunity to observe more details. The interior of Cain Master's home is simple yet elegant and updated, coupling the charm of an earlier time with the technological advancements of the twenty-first century. Hardwood floors line the entire house. The walls and trim are clean and off-white, the furniture both sturdy and understated. A large, wide-screen TV adorns a wall along with what looks like state-of-the-art intercom and alarm systems. In the kitchen, light blue and white tiles line the backsplash, setting off large stainless-steel appliances, while a massive digital calendar occupies one wall of the uber masculine room.

Fancy.

Every detail speaks of wealth and comfort. It's exquisite.

But the truth is, I'm more interested in the titles of the books on the shelves I see when I wander into the sitting room, little clues into the character of Cain Master. Most of these are in English, though I catch a few foreign titles. Many are the types of books you'd expect a well-read retired army general to read.

The Art of War.

Elemental Strategy.

The classics, some titles a bit surprising.

The Adventures of Tom Sawyer.

Cold Mountain.

Pride and Prejudice.

I've seen libraries like this before, outfitted with popular titles for show. But if you take a book off the shelf, you'll find the spine's never been cracked, the poor books left to collect dust. Not these, though. They're well-worn and clearly loved, every one of them bearing marks of repeated use.

Interesting. No e-book readers for Cain Master. Does he occasionally eschew modern technology, then? Or is there another reason for the volume of print books?

Footsteps sound in the foyer outside this sitting room, and I pause in my perusal. Is it him? But the footsteps retreat, along with the sound of a deep, masculine voice.

My pulse races. I don't recognize the voices as being from the night before, and for some reason, my intuition tells me they aren't the man I've come to see.

I twiddle my thumbs, read every title I can see in front of me on the lined shelves, then sit down and begin counting to twenty in every language I know. I'm at number ten in Hindi when footsteps approach, heading this way. I get to my feet. I know who it is.

A shadow precedes him. I still at his breadth and height just before he enters.

I know before he speaks, by the way the air seems thinner and the furniture somehow smaller... this is the master of the house.

He's taller than I am, by a full foot or more. Thick, dark brown hair just a touch longer than acceptable military length frames a ruggedly masculine face, his square jaw lined with stubble that underscores harsh, brutal beauty. If not for the cut of his jaw and the harsh lines of his face, he'd be too pretty.

He's younger than I expected. At least... physically.

His eyes tell another story.

They spark with latent energy and power. His posture commands respect, and swift, blind obedience, like the kings of old. I can't decide if I expect him to pull a sword out of a stone or bare his teeth with a show of fangs.

I meet his gaze, which is harder than it sounds, as it takes an act of sheer will not to look away. Stark, naked cruelty lies in the savage sapphire depths. Barely civil. He holds me in the power of that gaze for one wild, terrifying moment. A mere glimpse of the ferocious honesty in his eyes shows a world of barely contained fury and power, as if the blood of an unnamed god thrums in his veins, demanding homage and obedience before he snaps his fingers and orders destruction.

A shiver skates down my spine.

Heavy, dark brows slant over his eyes, and his mouth is a harsh slash softened by full lips. He stares at me, unblinking, his hands on his hips.

"May I help you?" I nearly startle at the rumble of his voice, as the polite words he's chosen bely a savage intensity I feel from across the room. He wears faded jeans and a black Henley, but the simple clothing doesn't hide the resilient cords of muscle that outline the column of his large neck and run down the nearly graceful slope of his powerful shoulders to the sleeves stretched tight across the carved biceps of his arms. His is a body perfected and honed for the sole purpose of harnessing a human's full potential.

I realize I'm not breathing, but it's his fault. He took all the air out of the room when he entered and barely left any for me. No fair.

He clears his throat, the polite veneer quickly vanishing, and I suddenly feel as if I've done something wrong. Have I? I suppose coming into his presence unbidden may qualify as unacceptable. Perhaps I was supposed to wait for a summons.

I brace myself, but he pauses, leaning casually against the side of an armchair. His voice drops an octave in warning. I haven't replied to him yet. Oops.

"Who are you?" His tone is accusatory, as if he only talks when necessary, and it's my fault I made him do it.

"Violet." I blink in surprise at myself. No one unnerves me. Why does he? With a deep breath, I stand taller and remember who I am. I square my shoulders and steady my voice. "Violet Price."

He doesn't respond. Normal people would say something forced but polite, like, "Pleased to meet you, Miss Price." But it seems he's already used up all his politeness for today.

"And?" His gaze no longer polite, his eyes scour the length of my body, lingering at the show of cleavage at my chest, moving quickly down my bare legs, then back to my face. He doesn't even pretend he didn't sneer at the dust on my shoes or my worn bag, or even bother to hide the fact that he just undressed me with his eyes, like it's his right because I'm standing on his property.

I should be offended. I should be angry that he just... *stares* like that. But I'm not. Instead, the deep, dark recesses of my mind beckon with a whisper.

God, what a man like him could do to a woman like me.

What I could do to bring him to his knees.

I don't like sex and never have, and yet...

Something tells me, he'd teach me how to enjoy it.

My cheeks feel hot. I clear my throat. It's time for me to take back control of this situation.

"Are you Mr. Cain Master?"

He nods, one brief jerk of his head. "I am." The sound of his voice feels like a liquid, sensual caress that skates across my naked skin, gently barbed with a prickle of heat.

I take in a deep breath. If he can skip the formalities, I can, too.

"Last night, my car was hit by someone I believe works with you. He totaled my car."

No show of surprise or reaction. No apology. He knows, then.

"Right," he says with a bored sigh. "You'll be fully compensated for any damages to your car or medical bills." He pushes off the side of the armchair and turns away from me. "Please leave your contact information before you leave."

I'm... dismissed?

He's given me the small amount of time he's reserved for interruptions, and now he has to go do manly, important, adult things.

How dare he?

"While I thank you for that, Mr. Master, covering damages caused by the guilty party is a given, and certainly not worth my time in coming to see you. Clearly, you're a man who values his time, so I won't waste it. That's not why I'm here."

He turns back to me, that fiery anger stoked in the depth of his eyes again with a warning I should heed. But there's something else I see that keeps my feet locked in place, holding me back from sprinting right out that door and leaving the way I came before he skins me alive.

He's curious.

Danger, my mind warns me. The man probably has enough room right here on this property to bury my body, and no one would ever even know.

Yeah, my mind went there, but after reading what I have about him, I can't help it.

His voice is a low rumble that borders on a drawl, challenging me.

"Then why are you here, Miss Price?"

The better question is, why does the way he says my name, drawing each syllable out like it's an act of foreplay, make liquid heat pool at my core? My skin shouldn't feel this tight. My breath shouldn't be this ragged.

"I looked you up when I got home. It started because I wanted more information about the man who hit my car, and what I found out about him led me straight to you."

Is that a glimmer of amusement in his eyes? No... it leaves so quickly, I wonder if I imagined it.

I clear my throat. I have his attention, so it's time I stop circling around him. It's time I go in for the kill. "And you're the man who could help me."

As he turns more fully to me, I watch the way his muscles bunch with tension. He raises his brows, a physical admission that I've interested him. When he crosses his arms over his chest, I realize he has muscles in places I didn't know even had them.

"Could I?" A low, lazy drawl.

This could be my only chance. I say it all in one breath, unblinking as I speak to him.

"I need your help to find the people I'm after."

God, I could've done better than that. They make it look so easy in the movies.

He cocks his head to the side, all traces of humor gone from his face. "And who are you after, Miss Price?"

I lower my voice as I stay my course. I've never been in the military, but something about his presence makes me speak to him as if I were. "That's a conversation for a much more private audience, sir." Though we're alone here, we both know anyone could walk in on us at any moment.

I want to bite the little nail of my pinkie on my left hand or tug a lock of my hair and fiddle my worry away, but I force myself to stand still and wait.

Several beats pass before he responds. Outside the window, his gardener walks by with a trowel and a rake. Far in the distance, the tide goes out behind him. I can almost hear the waves lapping at the shore.

"Let's take a walk." My heart flutters in anticipation. I'm a drowning woman, and he's thrown me a length of rope.

This is what I wanted, privacy with him, but a little warning voice in the back of my head tells me I should tell him no. I should talk him into speaking with me in his office or someplace neutral.

I came here for a reason, and I don't take no for an answer.

I go against my every instinct and follow him.

CHAPTER 2

Violet

IT ISN'T until we walk into the kitchen that I notice there are a lot more people here than I initially thought. Somehow, it helps me draw in a breath. They're just quiet, their presence and work seamless in the background. Two more of his staff are in the garden, and only paces away from them, four strong men dressed in military attire look like they're doing… drills? It's hard to tell from here, but it's clear they're training.

The guard at the door inclines his head at us as we pass, and Cain holds his palm up when he begins to follow us. Either he has guards outside as well, or he trusts that I'm not here to ambush him.

Maybe he shouldn't be so trusting.

The side door leading to the garage opens, and a portly, middle-aged Latina woman with pretty brown eyes and short brown hair enters, her arms heavily laden with brown grocery bags. Cain pauses, his hand on the door to exit, when he sees her coming in.

"You know better than to carry those in yourself," he scolds, clucking his tongue at her as he walks over to her. "Alma, why didn't you call me?" Reaching her, he plucks the bags out of her hands before sliding them onto the countertop.

She smiles at him. "Eh, thought you'd be busy, and it's good for me to still do things sometimes, *señor*," she says.

"And you're no good to me laid up in bed because you threw your back out again," he mutters, rebuking her. I nearly cringe at the sharp edge in his tone, but she only winks at me.

The door shuts behind us. The warm summer air tickles my skin.

"Mr. Master—"

"Call me Cain."

Skipping the formalities so soon. Interesting. "Cain. That's a unique name. I've only known one other man with a name like that, but he spelled it differently." The son of one of my foster parents.

"You've looked up my name."

"Of course." I am not going to lie to him unless I have to.

A shadow crosses his features for a split second before he grows serious. "You don't hear the name Violet every day either."

"My name was supposed to be Angela, but when my mother saw my eyes, she changed her mind."

"You were born with eyes that color, then?"

A curious question. It shouldn't please me that he's noted the color of my eyes. Everyone notices them, but *he* seems the type that only notices you if it matters.

"Yes."

We walk in silence down a path made of stones that leads past the garden to the barn or shed or whatever it is.

"I'm not going to waste your time, Mister—Cain. You own a private investigation agency."

He walks with his hands in his pockets, which might look casual but really only serves to make the muscles along his arms and neck bulge that much more. *God.*

"Depends on who you ask."

I have to walk faster to keep up with his long strides. I'm falling behind him. For one brief, crazy moment, I'm tempted to smack his back and tell him to slow down. "What do you mean?"

He shrugs a large shoulder and scowls at the path in front of him. "I don't advertise."

"And yet, I'd hazard a guess you're booked through next year."

"And then some."

We walk in silence for another moment while I try to formulate a plan to tell him what I need.

"I don't have the kind of money you'd ask for, but… I could barter."

Why did it sound so much better in my head?

He stops walking long enough to give me an amused smirk. "I don't need homemade soap or homegrown tomatoes." Another rude glance down at me. "And you're right. You can't afford my company." I know he means I can't afford to hire him, but the way he says it makes it sound like I'm not worthy of being in his presence. I bite the inside of my cheek so I don't tell him off, grounding myself in the stab of pain.

Deep breath in. Deep breath out.

My cheeks heat. I decide the best course of action is to ignore the taunt. "We could help each other. A mutually beneficial situation. I mean, I—I have talents and skills that could benefit your organization, and I could benefit from what you have to offer as well."

He sighs. "Don't waste my time. To be honest, I'm not even sure this consultation is something you could afford, but it's warm out and I needed some fresh air. I'd be charging most people by the hour for this discussion alone, but I'm taking pity on you." He looks down at my crumpled dress and faded purse. My skin prickles uncomfortably, but before I can respond he continues. "You're already talking about collaboration, and I don't even know why you're here."

I won't rise to take his bait, I *won't*. But God, my temper's a beast, and it's hard to keep it on a leash sometimes.

"I—I need help finding a few people, and I believe you could help me."

Still scowling, he doesn't respond, so naturally I feel the need to keep talking, because that always helps.

"I'm skilled in martial arts. I'm reigning champion on the East Coast—"

"In the women's division," he interrupts with an impatient sigh.

Does he know that? Does he know anything else about me, or was it just a guess about an obvious fact?

My blood begins to go from a simmer to a boil, and I slow my pace. "Excuse me?"

"In the women's division," he repeats with a casual shrug, hands still in his pockets. "Means nothing when you're up against a man."

"Oh, is that right?" *Chauvinistic prick,* I mentally tack on.

I imagine drop-kicking him right here. A swift kick between his legs would incapacitate him enough for me to move quickly.

He doesn't bother to hide the disdain in his tone. "Of course. I'm sure you could drop a pussy on his ass, but it means jack shit unless you're fighting a real man."

He's dropping all semblance of professionalism, and another warning bell chimes in my mind.

We've made it to the edge of the garden. A brisk wind carries warm air from over the sea, white-capped waves crashing in the distance behind him. A gull caws overhead, but I hardly hear it. The blood pounds in my ears with my rising temper. A corner of his beautiful, perfect lips quirks upward. Mocking me. "Got under your skin. Want to prove me wrong?"

I'm already in a fighting stance, my shoes kicked to the side like so much baggage. My hands clench into fists at my sides. I don't care who he is, he just tossed the gauntlet down and I *do not back down.*

"Of course I do."

Stop, the little inner voice of reason warns.

I never did like that voice.

And suddenly, it doesn't matter that I'm wearing a dress, that he's a hundred pounds heavier than I am, and I'm trying to convince him to hire me. All I see is a brawny sexist who needs to learn a lesson.

I've spent years perfecting the double-leg takedown, a move that works in the ring or on the street. If he was unaware, I might be able to take him down. He's prepared though, and way too big.

All I want to do is level him. I could drop him to the ground, without actually causing injury. I've done the move a thousand times. Though he's bigger than I am—by a lot—I'm smaller and more agile, giving me a decided advantage. But while it might be satisfying to drop a man of his size to the ground, that's just the problem—he's fucking huge, and I'm not, and that really fucking matters.

"No." With effort, I drop the fighting stance, and shrug my shoulders. I walk casually over to him. "You're too big for a girl like me," I say with mock humility. I wait until he resumes his casual walking. "I couldn't possibly—" He looks away from me, a strategic error and my only chance.

Thwack. I kick my leg out so fast I register surprise in his eyes, but he's even faster than I am. Instinctively, he deflects, and instead of striking back, ducks. When he's bent over, I shove, pushing him off-kilter.

For one second, one glorious second, I've got him as he's taken by surprise and falls. I quickly pin him down. Victory courses through me, and I can't stop the grin that sweeps over my face at the surprise in his eyes. But the moment's short-lived.

Fuck.

His eyes darkening to gray blue, he coils his body, and the next thing I know, I'm soaring through the air. There's an audible sound of a tear, and then… he's immobilized me.

No.

He's on top of me, and I'm pinned beneath him.

"You think you need to show me who you are?" he asks. Just to show off, the bastard's got both my wrists in one huge hand, and I can't move.

I realize three things at once.

First, my dress is torn. The ripping sound was the neckline. A flap of fabric moves in the breeze, baring my bra-clad boobs to him. *Great.*

Second, his… *body is on top of me.*

And he's… large, and strong, and masculine, and really smells a lot better than any man ever should. Images of the two of us naked flit through my mind because I'm not a corpse, and other than us not knowing each other, being outdoors where anyone could see us, and fully clothed… what's to stop me from mentally going there?

Third… he's furious. A vein throbs in his temple, and his nostrils flare. I can tell he's holding himself back from really hurting me.

My throat tightens with the sudden knowledge that once again, I've let my temper get the best of me and probably just ruined *everything*.

Again.

He won't let me stay now. I know he won't. Only a fool would.

"You were saying?" His eyes spark at me like flashes of flint.

"I can fight," I say through gritted teeth, my voice shaking.

"Of course you can." He spits out the words like venom. I feel momentarily vindicated. He doesn't wonder if I can fight. "*That* was never in question."

Wasn't it? Did he bait me? If he did, I leapt to it like a goddamn fish to a worm-covered hook. His admission that I can fight takes a bit of the wind out of my sails.

If I wasn't fully restrained under him, I could reach out and touch that rugged stubble along his jaw. There's a silvery scar near his left eye I didn't notice before, weirdly similar to mine. Huh.

"You listen." His voice is a deadly purr, like the growl of a mountain lion warning its prey. He lowers his face to mine so we're only inches apart. I can't believe I thought he had an ounce of softness in him just moments ago. He's nothing but hard lines and angles, as flexible as steel. A bead of sweat runs down the side of his face, but his eyes are cold as ice. "Do not *ever* do that again."

"Do what?" My voice is barely a whisper.

He leans in closer, the muscles along his neck taut. He bares his teeth, his voice no more than a growl. "Try to fight me."

He doesn't even say *fight me*, but *try*.

Ouch.

Okay, so I'm getting off with a warning? If he wanted to throw me off his property, he wouldn't use the word "again."

Would he?

He's got me in an expert submission hold, more skilled than most I've fought before.

I came here to suggest a business proposal and he's served me humble pie.

Good one, Vi. I stifle a sigh.

"Tell me you won't ever even think about fighting me again, Miss Price."

"I won't fight you." My voice is clogged with emotion. I don't concede often, and when I do, it's under duress, just like this. I don't make any promises beyond that, though.

There are many, *many* things I could do that don't fall under the umbrella of "fighting."

"Why are you here?"

"You're still on top of me."

"I'm aware." He doesn't budge.

I won't sugarcoat things. I won't pretend I'm here for any reason other than my true purpose. I draw in a breath and hold his gaze, unblinking, my tone of voice firm and confident despite my compromised position.

"I need you to help me find the people who killed my parents."

Still holding me beneath him, he gives me one short nod before he releases me. I get to my feet, shaking a little, and fruitlessly try to hold the flapping fabric against my breasts. My hands shake.

He reaches for the hem of his tee and yanks it up over his head before he tosses it in my direction.

Numbly, I catch it mid-air. It's soft and warm and smells like him, spicy and virile and all male.

I look at him and blink.

"Put it on."

I look down at my bare chest and ripped dress, then back like an idiot to the bunched-up fabric in my hand before I realize he's standing bare from the waist up in front of me. As he turns away from me, I tug the tee on quickly, to block my view of his perfect, chiseled back, crossed with the same silvery scars as my own.

For some reason, that makes me want to cry. No one has scars like that without a story. No one.

His tee swims on me, and I feel like an utter fool, the edge of my dress peeking out underneath the hem of his shirt. But I came here with a purpose, and I'm not leaving until I tell him more. So, I ignore the burning in my throat. I ignore the way his tee feels on me, too soft for a man like him, so warm it's a comfort. I ignore the way my body responds to his.

And I take back an ounce of control. I can either walk around here like a little kid wearing her brother's oversized tee, or I can own this.

I reach to the back of the dress, ignore the pain in my arm from the awkward position, and tug the zipper down. I shimmy out of it, and the ripped fabric pools around my ankles. I bend and lift it, so I'm wearing nothing but his tee like a dress.

If he's surprised, he doesn't show it, only crooks his finger at me. I follow.

I read once that in the animal kingdom, a female can't control the innate biological desire to mate with an alpha male. Instinctively, she knows he would protect her and their offspring

I comfort myself with the knowledge. Visceral attraction to an alpha male is an instinct, not a choice. It isn't my fault.

"Come with me." He jerks his chin forward and begins to walk. I'm not really a fan of being bossed around, but I think I've pushed my luck enough.

With his shirt flapping around my body, I follow him to the fence at the edge of his property. From here I can see he has a pretty, curved pool with a small waterfall cascading into it from the left. Adirondack chairs line the sunny perimeter, a perfect retreat.

"Sit."

He folds his bulk into a large chair by the poolside and jerks his chin at a chair opposite him. I choose a chair as far away from him as I can get. Here, I'm in direct sunlight and blinded, unable to stare at his muscled shoulders, the dog tags that swing around his neck, or those washboard abs I would drink shots off of and not regret. Even while staring at his eyes, I'm aware of a faint smattering of dark hair across his chest, the way his waist tapers to faded jeans that hug his waist right where… I swallow. And block out everything I can to focus on him.

I've studied neurolinguistic programming, among other brain tricks. If you train yourself hard enough, you can erase bad memories, traumatic events, and replace them instead with a flash of white or a happy thought. It takes practice, but it can be done. In a split second, I mentally block out his masculinity and focus on his eyes, the rest of him bathed in imaginary bright white.

"Tell me everything."

"About what?"

"About what you need from me."

I take a risk and push him a little.

"You've already decided I can't afford your services and you've already decided I'm of no use to you. So why tell you?"

A slight narrowing of his eyes tells me he isn't used to being questioned. "Did I say I have no use for you?"

Did I—does he mean—no. *God*, no. Again, I want to run, and again, I make myself stay before my mind thinks of the very many ways he can use me. "No, sir. You didn't."

"Then tell me. Let's just say I'm curious."

I know without explanation that the only way I'll ever get his cooperation and help is to do exactly what he's asking.

So, I do. I give him the bald, honest, painful truth. I tell him quickly and succinctly, so I don't waste his time or mine.

"When I was four years old, my father worked as an assassin. My mother did not know this, and it took me a full decade after I put my mind to it to find out the truth. One night, they were pulled from their beds and executed."

Anyone else would be surprised by this. It's not exactly a story you tell when you first meet someone. It's not a story *I* tell anyone.

I register no surprise in his eyes. He's heard accounts like mine before.

It's why I'm here.

"Whoever it was never came after me. We lived in a cramped apartment, and my makeshift room was a closet. My mother must've shut the door when she heard intruders."

"Sloppy work."

"At the very least, hasty. I spent the rest of my childhood in foster care until the moment I turned eighteen. I've been piecing things together about their death since my earliest memories, and I've reached an impasse."

"How old are you now?"

"Twenty-four."

He holds everything I've said for a moment and doesn't respond.

I watch as he crosses his ankle over his knee and leans back, lacing his fingers behind his head. I make my eyes look away from the rippling muscle he effortlessly flaunts when he leans back.

"And what will you do when you find them?"

"The same thing you would."

It's a bold move, to assume I know how he'd behave.

I brace myself for his anger, or outrage, or a command to leave. Maybe he'll even call someone to come and escort me off his property. How far is too far to push a man like him?

He does none of those things.

"And what is it I would do?"

I squirm but don't look away. "You'd kill them."

He doesn't deny it.

"I don't think you're capable of murder, Miss Price."

So, we're back to formalities. I can play that game, too.

"That's only because you don't know me, sir."

"And if I did?"

I swallow before I draw in a deep breath. "You'd know that there's nothing I won't do for the people I'm loyal to."

He slowly nods. The hint of approval fills me with pride.

Run, my instinct warns. It's dangerous to value the opinion of someone like him.

"That's closer."

"Closer to what?"

"Convincing me to hire you."

CHAPTER 3

Cain

SHE'S HERE. I've waited for this. I've planned this. And everything I've orchestrated led her here, but she can't ever know that.

I'll kill Armand for the way he did this. Fucking hit her car to get her attention, planted bits and pieces of information for her to find us. But it was too damn risky, the son of a bitch.

I look at the way she sits, her back ramrod straight in one of the pool chairs, my tee melting against her curves like a seductive tease.

It's a mistake to hire her.

I don't hire impulsive, headstrong people for my team.

Ever.

But that's not why I wanted her here.

She can't know why I'll hire her. Not now. Not ever.

I want Violet Price so close to me I could touch her. I know every goddamn thing about her. If she knew who I am and why she's really here, she'd run. Maybe even change her name again.

I've been obsessed with her for six months.

Who was the woman with the mesmerizing eyes? The first time I saw her, I wanted her. I had to have her. And I haven't gotten her out of my mind since.

I saw her in one of our surveillance videos. We were monitoring a local shopping mall, and her studio was doing a demonstration. Then there she was. Violet eyes staring at our camera as if she knew who we were, that we were watching her. We were trailing one of the parents in her youngest class, not her, and later found him guilty of cheating on his wife. The man was dumb enough to bring his girl-friend to a jewelry store at the mall. We pocketed half a million for that one.

We got what we needed the first two minutes into the surveillance footage. It was crystal clear. Yet I played that video over, and over, and over again until I could recite every line she said, make every move she made.

And I was obsessed.

I spent the next week learning everything I could about her, and finally had Armand put up video surveillance where she worked out. We stayed out of her home until last night.

I noted the way she held herself. When she wasn't throwing punches or kicks, she assumed a fighter's stance, light on her feet, knees slightly bent. The only move she made with more effort than the rest was blocking. *No one* hit her. Ever. She was a master at self-protection.

It wasn't until after my initial... obsession... that I unearthed her skillset.

Small and lithe, she's a fighter to the core. She can hold her own when she needs to, and she fucking will. Skilled in multiple languages, indefatigable, her only real flaw is disrespect for authority. It only draws me to her more, because I'll teach her that skill. On my terms.

With the exceptions of our doctor and on-site chef, every member of my team is ex-military. Dishonorably discharged. I like it that way, and I have my reasons. I, of all people, should know what it's like to have to defend your honor and fight for respect. I give my team that chance, and because I have, they're loyal to me.

Violet isn't.

How would I keep her loyal to me? She tells me she is, and I believe her. But talk is cheap. She'll have to show me with her actions that she means what she says.

I've never hired anyone like her, someone ruled by emotions instead of intellect.

But I'll make an exception for Violet.

It's her fire that fuels her, and *that's* what she'll learn to harness. To use. To finely tune into a weapon.

I planned it this way, her coming to me for help. I need what she has to offer, but on my terms and my terms only.

I push myself to standing from the chair, and I don't miss the way her eyes go a bit wider with fear, a sort of desperation surfacing that I know too well. She knows I'm about to dismiss her. That our meeting is over.

I have to. It's the only way to get her buy-in, to make sure she's as committed to our team as everyone else. If her place here is hard-won, I've got one more chance at ensuring her loyalty.

"Go home, Miss Price. Send a formal resumé to the address I'll give you. I have your contact information because of the accident. Now if you'll excuse me—"

The T-shirt of mine she's wearing billows in a gentle breeze from the water. She's a woman cut from marble and tough as nails, somehow made vulnerable in borrowed clothing. A gust of wind whips her hair around her face, the windswept look nearly shaking my resolve to dismiss her.

I don't want her to leave. She belongs here.

She shakes her head at me.

I blink in surprise.

"No?"

I don't realize I'm clenching my fists until I see her eyes quickly dart to where my hands curl by my sides.

"No, sir."

I'm so surprised I don't respond at first.

No?

I fully expected her to push back, to fight for what she wants. Hell, it's exactly why I'm giving her shit. But I didn't expect flat-out defiance. My voice sharpens.

"I don't hire people for my team who don't know how to respect authority, Miss Price."

I take a step toward her, and to her credit, she stands her ground.

"I know how to respect authority."

The waves behind her whip in a frenzy, whitecaps rising and crashing against rocks. Clouds roll in, the sky quickly darkening. A storm's brewing.

I don't have the time or patience for this.

"Bullshit. Words are cheap, Miss Price. You don't know the meaning of the word respect."

Her lips thin, as a wispy piece of hair crosses her vision. She pushes it impatiently out of the way. "I respect the authority of the people who earn it, Mr. Master."

Ah, so we're playing *that* game.

"If you think this is how a job interview is conducted, I'd suggest you go back to school."

"Job interview?" She shakes her head and actually laughs. "That was never in question. I'm no one's employee, Mr. Master. I'm suggesting I work for you as a paid contractor. Barter and trade, the very building blocks of modern-day free enterprise."

Well played.

She wears her defiance well, and it makes me goddamned hard.

What I wouldn't give to strip that all away from her, one stroke at a time.

I will.

"No."

She shakes her head from side to side. "No, what? No, bartering isn't a cornerstone of free enterprise? No, you won't work with me?"

When I was her age, I'd kill a man for less than this. I was paid to. I built my business on the back of those early days.

"Come here, Miss Price."

I don't forget the way it felt with her wrists trapped between my fingers, her pulse racing. I loved the feel of her beneath me, pinned under my weight and heaving for breath. She thought she'd best me, and she did catch me off guard, but not for long.

The first time I saw her, I knew that she was the one we're after—no, the one we *need*. I need. It was written in the way she held herself, in the rigidity of her spine, the tightness in her jaw.

I watched her fight.

Her hair caught back in a tight, merciless bun, she wore little to no makeup. It didn't matter. I knew I was looking at a goddamn masterpiece.

There's a slight scar across her left eyebrow, the only imperfection on her otherwise flawless face, the type of scar one gets from a street fight. There's a story behind that scar. I mean to find it out.

Violet Price is five foot even and one hundred ten solid pounds of muscle. Petite, but powerful, like tightly packed dynamite.

My T-shirt blows about her slight frame. The cool breeze from the ocean warns us a storm is coming, and fast, but she ignores her hair whipping around her with wild abandon. Her stunning eyes, a deep, mesmerizing hue, are like nothing I've ever seen before, so much more brilliant when I see her up close.

I want her closer.

Violet.

Amethyst caught in light. The color of magic.

It's both her name and her most distinguishing characteristic.

One of the few colors labeled by Newton when cataloging the spectrum of visible light, violet's the rarest of any eye color, so rare many believe violet eyes to be mythological. But no. Her violet eyes, those singular gems of beauty, are no myth, and they're staring straight at me. "Yes?"

It's on the tip of my tongue to offer half my kingdom for *one night* with her. One blessed, glorious night, and she'd be mine. All mine.

"You have a look on your face I'd pay good money to decipher," she says in a voice so low it's as if she's talking to herself.

Words spoken before a storm like this feel stealthy and classified, like the first brisk wind will sweep them away.

"Not sure you'd want to hear what I'm thinking right now."

"I definitely do, Mr. Master." She takes a step closer to me, her voice low. "Try me, sir."

"I'm thinking of the terms of our contract, the types of terms that professionals would never consider."

A beat passes. I watch as her tongue darts out and runs across her chapped lips. "Perhaps professionalism is overrated."

A whistle blows three times in succession. The spell is broken. My breathing stills. Even the breeze over the water seems to cease. I whip my head around to look at the house.

"It's an alarm," she says. "Isn't it?"

I don't respond.

The heavy sound of feet running toward the house comes from the training area. I listen, braced for the second alarm as I do a mental tally of all staff on hand. My men in training. Joe, Claude, Henri.

Violet.

The back door's yanked open, and Joe stands, barely visible under the shadow of the awning.

"What is it? Who sounded the alarm?"

"I did. When you didn't answer your phone, sir. It's Skylar."

Skylar? I can't be hearing him right. *Skylar?*

I know the answer to my question before I ask it. I'm not sure why I do. "Is it urgent?"

He winces, as if recoiling from an invisible blow. "She's missing, sir."

Storm clouds break open, and a torrent of rain sweeps down. I run for cover and barely catch myself from grabbing Violet's hand to tug her along with me. She doesn't need my help, but it's tempting. The only woman in my life who means something to me is in danger, and the frantic need to control something consumes me.

Violet isn't mine.

We're soaked before we get to the door.

I turn to Violet and note the desperation in her eyes. She wants this so badly, she's trembling.

I grab a fistful of dish towels from the kitchen drawer and toss them at her. Not missing a beat, she wipes her eyes and pushes wet hair out of her face. The straps of her heels are slung around one finger, and as we walk through the kitchen, she shoves her torn dress in the trash bin.

Change of fucking plans. If my sister's at risk, I need Violet's help, and I need it now. I wanted to recruit her for a purpose just like this, because I needed a woman on my team who could get shit done, and her list of qualifications outnumbers everything else.

"When can you start?"

She blinks. Her reaction will be telling. I note a flash of alarm that quickly fades to eager excitement. "Immediately."

"We negotiate terms of your contract with me today."

She nods eagerly. "Yes, sir."

"You start now, Miss Price."

CHAPTER 4

Violet

SKYLAR. I know enough about body language to know Skylar is someone who matters to him. He moves like he's at war, preparing for an ambush, and whoever's responsible for hurting Skylar's going *down*.

Yikes.

Who is it? An ex? I doubt she's a current girlfriend or significant other. He's the type that would want a woman who mattered to him nearby, under his protection and watchful eye. I haven't missed the way his team trains right here on his property.

I go through a myriad of feelings at once.

Elation—*he hired me!*

Fear—*will this go the way I planned?*

Panic—*what does this mean? What's happened to Skylar?*

He walks at a clip I have to run to keep up with, either oblivious or unconcerned with my trailing behind him. I don't mind it, though. Moving fast burns the adrenaline that courses through me like fire.

When we reach the house, a tall, lanky man with a shaved head comes out. Two meaty pit bulls circle Lanky Man's legs, prowling as if they smell the blood of someone new in their territory.

My heart swells. God, I love pit bulls. What most people don't know about them is that they used to be nanny dogs, hired to watch over and protect babies and small children. A cross between terriers and bulldogs, pit bulls were once used as symbols of American strength during the First World War.

They're fiercely loyal and protective to a fault, though. And once trained to guard illegal activity, drug dealers and the like used them for their own benefit. When they attack, they don't let go. They'll bite to kill. And while that might've once kept children safe, pit bulls have gotten a bad rap in recent years.

I love them. I want to kneel in front of them and nuzzle their chocolate-brown necks and scratch their perky ears.

I've always been attracted to powerful, lethal creatures.

. . .

"Just got a call from Lottie."

Cain nods. "And?"

"Said she never came home last night. They expected her at midnight, and when she didn't show, they figured she was spending the night with her date."

His jaw clenches, but he doesn't otherwise react. "And?"

"And when she didn't come home this morning, Lottie got scared. Said she didn't know what to do or how to reach her, and thought you'd want to know."

"I would've wanted to know last night," he says through gritted teeth.

I'm glad I'm not the one on the receiving end of that anger. It boils at a low simmer, threatening to scald and eradicate anything it touches.

"Right, sir, but you were traveling, and not even due back until today."

Cain curses under his breath, then turns and jerks his chin at me. "You. Come with me." Like I'm going anywhere else? I'm wearing his damn T-shirt, and he just hired me. If he gave me a cot to sleep on, I'd camp right here.

I thought there were a lot of people around his house before. Now, it seems like people that work for him come out of the damn woodwork. Big, muscled guys. A few in military fatigues and others in civilian clothing mill around the large house, talking in hushed tones. None of them speak to Cain, and it takes me a minute to realize the reason they don't is because they're waiting for his command.

"Who's Skylar?" I ask, panting as I follow him up the steps two at a time.

His jaw tenses before he responds.

"My sister."

Oh, wow. Shit. Now *that* didn't show up in the search history. And why is a part of me relieved she's family, that she isn't a woman he has romantic ties to? My gut reaction spells danger, but I shove it down. I'll deal with that later. Now, I've got shit to do.

His sister… Has everything I read about him been a lie? Do I really know anything about him at all?

He shoves open the door to his office, and I'm not surprised by the way it looks. His desk is large, sturdy, and intimidating, a paragon of masculinity… just like him. Massive windows look out at the pool below, and on another wall one overlooks the waterfront view. Storm clouds gather to block the sun, darkening the room even though it's still daytime. He flicks on a switch, and bright overhead lighting illuminates the room.

"Sit."

He gestures for me to take a seat across from him.

Why me? Why now? Doesn't he have anyone else that works for him that could do whatever it is he wants me to do?

Lanky follows us into the room.

"Joe, meet Miss Price, our new hire."

I give him a little wave. "Hey."

Joe takes a seat beside me and leans forward, elbows on his knees.

Cain pulls out his phone and swipes. A grid shows up, with a little squiggly arrow, and he curses under his breath. "It shows her home, and it shows she hasn't left since Wednesday. That can't be right."

Joe shakes his head. "I was worried about this."

Cain blows out a breath. "Cut the shit, Joe. You don't have to be polite. You not only worried about this, you warned me about this. Said she wouldn't go for it."

I gather up my courage and clear my throat. They both look at me. "If I'm working for you, it would be helpful if you could fill me in a little?"

Joe looks to Cain for permission, and when he gets it, he nods. "Skylar's his younger sister."

"Got it. How old is she?"

"Only eighteen."

I cringe. Anything could've happened to an eighteen-year-old. She could've hung out at some guy's house and drank the night away, be still wrapped up in his sheets and not bothering with the time. She could've lost her phone or hooked up with someone and decided a trip to Vegas would be a smart idea. Really, anything goes.

Joe continues. "We put tracking software on her phone, because Cain wanted to keep an eye on her."

"Are you her guardian?"

A muscle tenses in his jaw. "No."

"Does she know you track her?"

"Found out two weeks ago."

"And lemme guess. Wasn't too fond of her big brother keeping tabs on her anymore?"

He huffs out a breath. "How'd you know?"

I nod. "It's kind of a given."

"Yeah, so she took all tracking off her phone..."

"But you're not dumb enough to really not keep tabs on her."

People frown all the time, a common facial expression one might say. When Cain Master frowns, the temperature in the room shifts, and my skin prickles. "Of course not."

He flips open his laptop, and the screen flashes to life. Cameras outside of a coffee shop show people entering and exiting with paper bags and steaming cups of coffee. Another camera shows the inside of a typical college kid's apartment, complete with beer cans stacked in blue plastic recycling bins, empty pizza boxes, and about ten pairs of shoes scattered haphazardly around the couch.

"Her place?"

"Yeah."

"She know about those cameras?"

He scowls at me. "What do you think?"

It's a rhetorical question, but I want in on this case, so I jump right in as if he really wants to know what I think. "I think you need to talk to her roommate and get everything she knows. Find out where she was last, who she was seeing, if she had plans. And I think you need to call the police."

The last suggestion was a test.

"You were spot on until you got to the police."

He passed the test. Still, I need to needle him a bit to get to more of the truth.

"You're not going to report a missing person?" *Le gasp. Oh, my, Mr. Master, are you above the law? Don't trust our criminal justice system? ::Hand to brow::*

"Lottie already did," Joe says with a scowl. "Police say she's not a missing person until she's been gone for twenty-four hours and wouldn't listen to her impassioned plea about why this was a special case."

"Right."

He scrubs a hand across his brow and shoots Cain a furtive glance before he looks back at me. "And if you're working with us, you might as well know as soon as they find out who she is, they won't touch it anyway."

I exhale. They don't know Candi, but something tells me I should tell them. "Just so you know, my best friend's an officer."

Again, no register of surprise. Either the man has an ironclad poker face like nothing I've ever seen before, or he already knows what I'm telling him. Great. Not a big fan of either of those options.

He's back on his laptop, swiping at the board. "I'll fill you in as quickly as I can. There will be time for more questions later, but we don't fuck around with this."

"Understood."

"Skylar was my mother's youngest child. My mother remarried when I enlisted in the army."

If he enlisted right out of high school, that puts him probably somewhere in his mid-thirties. My instincts tell me that if he'd reached seventeen or eighteen years of military service, he'd be almost untouchable, and very unlikely dishonorably discharged.

He pushes up from the table and stalks over to a large, framed print on the wall. He moves it to the side magically, like it's cast beneath a spell, before he punches in a code.

"Under normal circumstances, we'd have a training period, then initiation. No time for that, so you'll work with me and I'll fill you in as we go. We have an armory here at the house, but I keep some things personally locked up. My team knows I have this here and has the code. No one else knows and I'd like to keep it that way." He pauses, glancing at the ragged, soaked tee that clings to my body like plastic wrap. I nod and will myself not to be embarrassed by my total lack of clothing. I need gear.

He spits out words like they're bullets. I know he's concerned about his sister but I can't help wondering if I bring out his anger, too. "You're part of the team, but you'll have to earn your place. Going forward you'll keep a change of clothes on site. Am I clear?"

That gets my hackles up, and I inwardly cringe. Earn my place, like a dog begging for his table scraps? We'll see about that. I play nice, though. "Yes, of course."

I watch as he slides a handgun into a concealed holster at his waist.

"Do you know how to use a gun?"

Shit. My silence is response enough. He curses under his breath.

"You may be a skilled fighter, Miss Price, but you'll need something to keep you safe at long range. For now, you'll stay with me and have a guard on you, but you'll join me at the shooting range when they open tomorrow morning."

"Which is...?"

"Five o'clock."

"In the morning?"

He gives me a withering look and doesn't reply.

Five in the morning?

"How did you get here?"

I have a sneaking suspicion he knows but wants everything out in the open.

"I got a ride." I bite my tongue so I don't snap back to remind him it's his employee's fault I don't have a car.

"Right. I'll make sure you get one back, and you'll need a car."

Wow, okay then. "You don't have to give me a car as part of our arrangement—"

"I do. All my employees need reliable transportation. It's for my own peace of mind more than anything." His voice sharpens. "I won't have people that work for me taking a fucking Uber to work."

Ouch.

I need to remind him of something, though. "I'm not your employee, Mr. Master."

He purses his lips and doesn't reply, but I can feel the judgy judgment in the air. *Grrr.*

We're walking at a good clip, and he shouts out commands as we go. He tells one guy to run surveillance at the college (I'm guessing the one his sister goes to?), another to load "Goldie" with ammo (Who is Goldie and why does she need ammo?), and a third to keep a watch on all video surveillance of Skylar. Joe takes off.

He pulls out his phone and barks out a few commands.

As we walk through his house, as people dressed in fatigues start moving and calling him *sir,* it doesn't feel like a home but a compound or a military base.

At the door, Joe comes up to us with a folded pile of clothing and hands it to me.

"Take those with you," Cain orders.

With me? What the hell?

He looks up at Lanky—er, Joe. "Have Claude track my location and copy everything we say and do. No one follows us. I do not want backup until I call for it, is that clear?"

"Yessir."

He clicks a key fob, and bright lights and a beep light up a truck a few yards away from us.

Oh my God.

When I was a teen, I had a few friends who got their licenses, and everyone wanted a car. Some just wanted a set of wheels to get from point A to point B, some freedom and independence. Some wanted a nicer car that would take them to job interviews or on road trips.

I wanted a truck. Specifically, a Toyota Tundra 4WD with a crew cab and thirty-eight-inch mud terrain tires with eighteen-inch Rockstar rims.

Cain Master drives my dream truck.

His truck's like him, sturdy and fearless, a veritable force of nature. The wheels alone come up to my chest. *Good God*. Two-tone black rawhide leather seats with red inlay matches the candy blood-red paint job, and if it wasn't for Massachusetts' insanely strict gun laws, this baby would house a gun rack in the back perfect for a twelve-gauge shotgun or semi.

And is that... *no*. Behind this truck, in the back, there's an even bigger truck.

"You do not drive a Ford 650!"

He gives me a curious look. "I do, but it's too big to take tonight."

"Will you let me touch it? Please? I just want to touch it, just once."

Cain's lips twitch, and he mutters, "That may be crossing a line, Miss Price."

I don't dignify his response with a reply, and don't speak because I don't trust my voice.

"Not now." He's right, I know he is. We have to get moving. Still, one day I just want to sit in that beautiful truck.

I hoist myself up on the metal platform of the Toyota. I want to get into the cab before he notes how small I am compared to this thing and decides to do something drastic and chauvinistic like touch me and help me in.

He's your boss, I remind myself. Your ridiculously hot, very scary, very dominant alpha male boss who just joked about…

No, wait. Not boss. *Not boss.*

Business associate or…something.

Whatever.

I hop in so quickly I manage to smash my shins on the unyielding metal step. Fuck, that'll bruise. I don't wince or say a word but silently slide onto the passenger seat. He, naturally, swings himself in with one smooth motion like this truck was custom-built to accommodate him.

I take a quick look at the clothes in my hands. Some kinda faded khaki pants that could be men's or women's, but there's an adjustable waistband and elastic to help them fit. A small black tank top, pair of socks, pair of boots.

He stares down at the boots. "Those are the smallest size we had, but something tells me you'll still have to stuff them."

"I'm not *that* small."

It's a stupid thing to say when I'm sitting next to a man so big he could double in Green Giant ads. His hands are three times the size of mine, his arms bigger than my thighs, and *those* aren't even the most intimidating things about him. Normal humans are composed of skin and tissue and strung together with muscle. Cain defies normal human body structure, because every inch of him seems to be nothing but raw, corded muscle. If we broke down, I feel as if he could hitch this truck to his shoulders and haul us home without breaking a sweat.

"I'd guess you're five feet tall, just over a hundred pounds."

"Didn't anyone ever tell you it's rude to ask a woman her weight?"

I sigh. Exactly one-ten the last time I checked.

"I'm not asking. My point is, you're small. Pointless trying to argue."

He revs the engine, and heat pulses low between my legs. If this truck proposed to me, I'd accept. *Gah.*

"It can come in handy, you know," I say in protest.

"What can?"

"Being small."

He shifts in his seat and mutters to himself, "Could be a fuckin' issue, too."

"Not like I can help it."

He doesn't respond but launches straight into giving me more details about his sister. "Things to know. Skylar has the shittiest taste in boyfriends and won't ever bring them to meet me for dinner or anything before she dates them."

"Does that surprise you?"

He pauses, flicking on his directionals before he takes a turn, then cruises back up to a breakneck speed. I guess not only does he not have a use for the police, but he obviously seems to think they can't touch him.

"No."

"If I had a brother like you, I don't think I'd bring my skinny little boyfriends home to roast marshmallows by your bonfire either."

A glimmer of something like amusement flits across his face, but he quickly goes back to the scary mask.

He grunts. "Especially the kinds of assholes she dates."

"Okay, so this is important information to note if I'm going to help you with this investigation. Little sis dates assholes."

He nods. We've left the shore and are heading into the heart of the city. I love Salem, with its aged houses and history. As we leave the shore, we draw closer to the historical parts of Salem—the Witch House, other museums, and the House of the Seven Gables.

"Skylar wrote to me when I was stationed in Europe and didn't travel much. Didn't like coming home, didn't prioritize it."

Why didn't he like coming home? My radar pings again, adding to my growing list of *things I need to find out about Cain Master*.

"Well, I know how that goes," I say softly, almost to myself. I do. Some of us would give anything to never come home again. "You and Skylar. How close are you?"

"Pretty close. She wrote to me constantly when she was a kid and I was deployed. Slowed when she got older, but I still have those letters."

I nod.

"Right. When I got back… she lived at my place for a time. She got tired of finding my mom passed out on the couch or her flavor of the week in her bedroom. I was beyond done with it. She stayed here a few months. She needed some structure, guidance. I gave her that."

Yeah, I *bet* he's good at giving people structure and…guidance. I stifle a shiver.

I note how he chooses his words carefully but doesn't sugarcoat a thing, a master at precision in his speech.

"She wanted to date." He spits out the words like they're distasteful. "She was old enough to. Let's just say we didn't see eye to eye when it came to who she chose to date."

I nod. "Let me piece this together, then. She's raised by a mom who let her do whatever she wanted. Doesn't get what she needs. You went off and enlisted which gave you the structure and accountability *you* needed. She had none of that, so when you came back, you did your best to provide that for her." He nods. "She wasn't too fond of your rules and expectations, but she was maybe grateful for a roof over her head and a large, scary big brother who'd keep her safe."

He draws in his breath with practiced patience and gives me a look I can only classify as a warning. "Yeah."

"So she rebelled. On the one hand, wanted your protection and everything you could offer, but on the other, didn't like being treated like a child and wanted you to damn well know that."

"Right."

"So at the first chance she got, when her friends got an apartment, she took off. Maybe checked in with you from time to time but didn't do much more than that."

"Very good, Miss Price."

"I got the basics then."

"Enough chitchat. That more or less brings you up to speed. Two boyfriends ago, she dated a guy who told me, I shit you not, that he was leaving that night to go become a vampire. And the next one after that came wearing a fucking cape and black boots. In July." Something tells me he wouldn't forgive black boots and a cape even in the dead of winter.

"We *do* live in Salem."

He huffs out a breath.

"And… let me guess… she didn't bring anyone else to see you after that?"

He grunts like a caveman. I'd pay good money to hear what he said to those two boyfriends.

"Cape. Boots. Salem. Is your sister involved in anything with witchcraft? Wiccan?"

His back goes so rigid, I could trace a straight line from the top of his spine to his seat. "Yeah."

But he doesn't offer any other details.

"How so?"

"What do you mean?"

"Is she actually Wiccan?"

I watch his reaction. He looks like he wants to wince, but he catches himself. Instead, his fingers tighten on the wheel, his knuckles white. He does not like that his sister's involved with the crowd she is, not one little bit.

"Involved in witchcraft?" He makes a face like he just ate a rotten apple. "She's got friends that do it, but…"

Aww. Is the big bad alpha too scared to admit his sister's involved in something outside his control?

"Are you in denial about her involvement, Cain?"

His eyes narrow on the road ahead of him, but he still manages to give me a brief sidelong look. "Be careful, Miss Price."

Something in me thrills at the warning he gives me, my skin prickling with heat. His voice has dropped, and is it my imagination, or has the inside of this car just heated up about twenty degrees?

"Careful about what?"

"Treading into areas you know nothing about."

I release a breath patiently. "Mr. Master, if I'm going to work with you, it doesn't make sense for you to hold anything back from me."

He gives me a sharp, sideways glance before he looks in front of him again. "You'll help me find my sister. You'll help me make sure she's safe and that the idiots she shares living space with haven't done something brainless like sign her up to be sacrificed to their fucking gods for the summer solstice."

"They can't do that."

"Why not?"

"It's August. Summer solstice is in June."

I think I actually see little tendrils of smoke come out of his ears.

Easy, Violet. Don't poke the bear too hard.

"You think you're clever, don't you?" He shakes his head as he flicks on his directionals again and takes a left so hard, I swear the tires leave the ground for a fraction of a second, a hard feat considering what this monstrosity weighs. When my stomach settles back to where it should be, I remember to protest.

"I—"

"You think you have it all figured out. I'm an overprotective brother who doesn't know jack shit about teens and boyfriends and how to *relate*."

Well... If the shoe fits...

"What you don't know is that I goddamn know what it's like to be the ostracized freak who can't rely on his parents. I know what it's like to want to fit in, to find a peer group you can socialize with who'll value you for who you are, not what you do."

Oof.

"So yeah, maybe it looks like I don't have a lot of respect for this witchcraft thing. And maybe I don't. I value what I can see. What I can hold. What I can touch."

I nod. It takes me a few seconds to realize I'm clutching at my neck, like he's a vampire who's going to bite me. My blood thrums through my veins, hot and visceral, and my skin feels too tight. I have to get control of the situation. He continues.

"I don't have a lot of use for bullshit. I will find the truth if I have to hunt it into dark valleys and hold it at knife point. Do we understand each other, Miss Price?"

I draw in a breath and release it slowly as I unfold the clothing in my lap. "Perfectly, sir." I cast a glance around the small interior of his truck. "Now where am I supposed to be getting dressed?"

CHAPTER 5

Cain

"Right here. I'm not looking."

Like fuck I'm not. I notice everything about her, from the way her fingers graze the pulse at her neck, to the wispy ringlets of hair that cling to her temple, still damp from the sudden summer shower that caught us unawares. I'm aware of her delicate scent, clean and fresh yet feminine, like moon-kissed dew. I'm aware that despite her training and level of fitness, of how easily I could hurt her.

I remember the way she felt pinned beneath me, how I held my weight above her so I wouldn't hurt her, both wrists gathered in my hand.

I remember how I liked it.

"Be quick about it, we're five minutes out."

"Not a problem."

She unfolds the tank, then wriggles it through the collar. Holding my T-shirt over her like a tent, she shimmies and wriggles and huffs into the clothes. If I wasn't so pissed and ready to kill, I'd find it amusing. Less than a minute later, she tosses the wet tee on the dash. I glance at her. She's dressed, and the clothes don't fit her well, but they'll stay on her for now. Next, she pulls the socks and boots on.

"We'll arrive in two minutes. We'll question everyone who's there and get all the details we can. What languages do you speak, Miss Price?"

"I'm fluent in French, Italian, German, and Japanese. I can get by in Portuguese and Russian, though don't ask me to write either."

She's being modest. She also knows passable Greek and Hindi as well.

I'm fucking hard just listening to her list some of her many talents.

"Noted. We'll get into why I hired you later, but for now I want you to know that I needed a woman on my team. There are places a petite woman like you can fit a lot more easily than a man like me or many on my team, and your skill set will also come in handy."

She nods.

"When you're proficient with a gun, you'll conceal and carry."

"Don't I need a license?"

"I'll take care of it. For now, if we get into a dangerous place, you'll use the skills you already have, but only at my command. You do *not*, under any circumstances, act without my permission."

"I thought we were just going to investigate."

"We are. I like to be prepared. Lesson one, Miss Price. Investigations can turn sour, and easily."

She nods, frowning as she looks out the window. "Why are the streetlights on during the day? That's odd."

I look to where she does. Each streetlight glows with a dim yellow light. I mentally commend her for noticing a detail I didn't. One of the reasons I hired her.

I flick a button on my phone. Joe answers immediately.

"Boss?"

"Check the electric grid between North and Downey Road. See if you notice any unusual activity."

I hang up the phone. I turn to Violet and point toward a sheathed knife on the console. "Have you ever used a knife?" I know for a fact she has, it's one of the many skills her studio has taught her that they don't advertise.

Though she doesn't answer me at first, I can tell just by the way she takes the ankle sheath she's skilled in knife use. In seconds, the sheath's safely secured under her pant leg, but easy to retrieve at a moment's notice. Throwing knives are long and sharp, and this one is no exception.

"Knives and I are BFFs, you could say."

We'll work on honesty, a two-way street. Eventually I'll tell her exactly why I've watched her and looked into her past. My reasoning is pretty simple and honest, but I know that if I tell her too much too soon, I could push her away. I can't risk that, not now.

I try to discreetly watch as she gets out of the cab of the truck, but I had nothing to worry about. She swings herself down like an expert, with grace and fluidity. Perfect. Something tells me I won't regret hiring her.

We walk at a good clip to Skylar's apartment building, but Violet pauses just outside the door. "Wait!"

I tamp down irritation. I don't like waiting, and I want to get this done. But she's fallen to one knee outside the door. She reaches out, fingering something I don't see right away.

"What is it?"

She shakes her head. "Flowers."

"Right. I'm sure there are flowers everywhere. I don't want to waste any—"

"No. No, listen." She stands, holding a delicate spray of tiny white flowers. "Baby's breath. I found the same flowers outside my car yesterday, these and a little purple one. Before I got into the accident."

"Coincidence?"

Her gaze is troubled when she looks at me. "Could be. We should note it, though."

"Noted. Now can we move on, please?"

My phone rings. Joe.

"Yeah?"

"Someone fucked with the electricity on that block last night. There are reports of the lights going off from dusk to this morning, and since they're set on auto, they came back on this morning when they don't usually."

"Thanks." I tell Violet, who only frowns but nods.

"Do you have like a special bag or something to hold evidence? We should maybe—"

I do not have the time or patience for this.

"For fuck's sake, stuff them in your bra if you're that worried." I turn to the door and push the doorbell. Out of the corner of my eye, she makes a gesture that *could* be flipping me off, but when I look sharply back at her, she shrugs her shoulders at me innocently. Probably just as well. Hauling her over my knee to teach her respect probably wouldn't go over too well right now.

The flowers are gone. I wonder if she took my advice. I imagine them pressed up against her perfect breasts, and with effort, pull my mind back to the job.

I turn back to the door at the sound of footsteps heading our way. Like many apartment buildings in downtown Salem, the door and stoop are aged with time and wear. A potted plant, the leaves dried and dead, sits to one side of the stairs. Below us, on the ground, my eyes fall on a crumpled condom. I hate that Skylar lives here.

Someone speaks to us through the door. "Who's there?" Lottie.

"Cain, Skylar's brother. Open up, please." The *please* is an afterthought. I try to remember my manners. Manners can sometimes get you places, but they're damn inconvenient.

Hushed voices rise and fall on the other side. Violet and I look at each other in silence as the door stays shut.

She shakes her head. "Now remember, you can't just go in there and kill them," she says in a whisper so soft I can barely hear her. I didn't even realize my hand was already grazing the butt of my gun. It's a little scary how she reads my mind.

"Why not?" I whisper back. I've killed for less than this, and I'd do it again. This is my sister we're talking about, my goddamn sister, and if anyone hurts her—

"Laws," Violet whispers. "You're no good to your sister in jail or dead yourself."

"Fucking logic." She can try all she wants, but she won't stop me if anyone's hurt Skylar. No one will.

I turn back to the door and raise my hand to knock, when I hear the clicking of metal, and the doorknob turns. Lottie, my sister's roommate and best friend, stares at me with wide, haunted eyes behind thick glasses. Her purplish black hair's in braids on either side of her head, and she wears a black cape with a black and silver dress over her curvy body. Someone I've never seen before—man or woman, I don't know yet, dressed in drab black clothing with long dark hair— stands next to her.

Lottie's voice is pained. "I didn't do it, Mr. Master. I had nothing to do with it."

Never a good way to begin a conversation.

"Do what?" I just want to get inside so I can ask some questions. I take a step toward her, and she steps back. Violet watches us both curiously.

"Any-anything." She's terrified of me.

Sometimes, that works against me. Sometimes it's in my favor.

I consider shoving past them to get inside, demanding answers to questions and scouring the place for clues, but I know that brute force isn't *always* the best response.

I look to Violet, and with subtle eye movements and a slight jerk of my head, silently ask her to get us in here without someone shitting their pants.

She steps forward, a smile on her lips.

"We didn't think you were to blame." Her voice exudes confidence and grace. She looks so small, so wholesome, no one would realize how quickly and easily she could cut or maim them. Her voice gentled, she stands close to me, as if showing with her physical presence that she's with me, and we mean no harm. "We're concerned, though, and want to help. Let us in, please?"

Lottie releases a breath, steps aside, and beckons for us to go in.

The sweet, nearly acrid smell of incense hits me when we set foot inside. It's hard to tell it's daytime, with the blinds drawn and nothing but candles lighting our way. Several cats curl around my ankles before gracefully gliding away. I take in every detail I can. Skylar's never invited me, but I've had surveillance on it since she came here. I know the basic layout, but now I'm looking for other details.

It's a small, crowded apartment. Two bedrooms? The kitchen sink is tidy but cluttered, dishes stacked on a drying rack that's nearly bursting. Beside the dishes there's a stack of coffee mugs, Zodiac signs engraved on the outsides of them. A velvet cushion lies on a table to the left, and several long, carved sticks that look like wands sit atop it. A carved structure featuring three women in dresses, holding hands around a white candle base, sits to the left of the cushion with the word *goddess* engraved below, and beside the candle a long incense burner casts smoke heavenward. The scent grows stronger.

On one wall several silver pendulums hang on a silver peg, and in the living room, there's a stand with a large, clear sphere. A crystal ball? Several dragons are displayed on the walls, some carved in 3D and some flat prints. The door to one bedroom's ajar, revealing an unmade bed and a large stack of unfolded laundry in a wicker basket. One of the cats walks into the room, quickly swallowed up by darkness.

"Miss Price, meet Lottie. Lottie, Miss Price. Lottie's Skylar's best friend and roommate."

"Pleased to meet you." Violet sticks her hand out, but Lottie doesn't take it. She stares at her, untrusting.

I turn to her companion. "And you are?"

"Haven, my boyfriend," Lottie says. He gives me a jerky nod, then steps back, falling into the shadows. Can't speak for himself? Interesting. I turn back to Lottie.

"You called us. What has you concerned?"

Lottie wrings her hands and paces in front of me. "Skylar had a date. Someone we met at a local gathering."

Gathering. What exactly is a gathering? I do my best to reserve judgment, but it's hard, seeing the dark, cramped apartment my sister shares with her friends, knowing I'm fully capable of putting her in a bigger, better place.

"They were supposed to go to dinner," Lottie says. "They had plans, and she even told me where they were going." Tears brim behind her glasses.

"Where?"

"Bubbles and Broomsticks." Pretty common name. In a city like Salem, over a quarter of the local establishments features names playing off some variation of the word "witch."

"She went to meet him, and she came home earlier than she expected. She'd texted me that the guy creeped her out."

"Did she give you specifics? What exactly creeped her out?"

I fucking hate that my sister went out on a date with someone she didn't trust and I didn't know.

I pace in the kitchen, trying to ignore the way I want to break things. My hands clench, and I try to steady my breathing. I hate this. If they hadn't tampered with anything, I'd have gotten full footage of everything. "And I have no idea where she is because you two thought it smart to remove all surveillance."

Violet places a gentle hand on my arm. My skin heats where she touches me, and I take in a calming breath. My fingers unclench, relaxing by my sides.

I didn't know she'd have that effect on me.

Lottie doesn't respond but plays with a silver lip piercing, her brows drawn together over her large glasses.

"What happened after she came home?"

"Well, about an hour later, I heard the front door open and close again. I yelled after her, but either she ignored me, or she didn't hear me. Honestly either could've happened."

"Did you see her?" Violet asks.

"When she came home?"

"Yeah."

Lottie shakes her head.

"So she didn't respond, and you didn't see her," Violet says. "Is it feasible that it was someone else who came into the house and left again?"

Lottie's magnified eyes widen. "Oh. Oh, God, I didn't think of that."

"Do you lock your door?" Violet asks, shooting me another look as if to warn me not to lose my shit.

"Well… sometimes, yes, sometimes no."

Even Violet looks frustrated at this point. "Lottie, this is important. Did you lock the door last night?"

Lottie winces. "I have no idea."

Violet's lips thin. I run my thumb over the metal handle of my gun to calm my nerves.

"So she probably didn't come home," I supply.

"No."

Lottie's companion shifts on his feet, as if enduring something uncomfortable.

Violet keeps her voice gentle. "What makes you think she didn't just go back out with him? Why call us?"

She turns to face me. "She left her phone here. She didn't tell me where she was going. And that on its own might not have really concerned me. But we have a rule, we always tell each other where the other's going."

The one smart fucking thing she's told me today.

"I'm going into her room," I tell Lottie over my shoulder, halfway in.

"Mr. Master, I don't think that's a wise idea—"

I ignore her. Violet walks in behind me and voices my thoughts when she looks around the room.

"Oooh. Oh my."

The gauzy black curtains are drawn over the windows, but it isn't dark enough to hide the large, king-sized bed decorated with a circular, plush blanket in purples and blacks, the skeletons that dance along every flat surface in a macabre display, or the feathery dream catchers that hang from the ceiling. That isn't what's got my attention, though, nor Violet's.

A curved, black leather chair sits in one corner of the room.

"Is that what I think it is?" I say out of the corner of my mouth to Violet.

"A chair designed for tantric sex and multiple positions or partners?" Violet responds. "Ohhh yeah."

I curse under my breath. "And you know this because…"

"I believe that question violates our confidentiality agreement, Mr. Master."

"We don't *have* a confidentiality agreement, Miss Price."

Her tight-lipped smile makes me want to smack her saucy little ass.

She steps further into the room and looks around. "Something for sure's off," she says. "Look."

She points to where Skylar's phone sits, plugged into the wall. Her laptop's beside it, and the little bowl for her cats is empty. "No way she'd leave without putting fresh water and food out for her pets."

Lottie stands in the doorway. "And you called the police?"

"I did." She sighs. "They won't touch the case. They said that she hasn't been missing long enough and we have no evidence."

What she doesn't say is that knowing I'm Skylar's brother doesn't help the situation.

Violet's frowning, my sister's phone in her hand. It's password-protected, and she hasn't gotten far with it.

"We're taking this with us," she says. "I'm sure I'll be able to get in."

Lottie doesn't protest.

Moons line every surface of the room. Half-moons pinned to the wall with Latin phrases I don't know, a full moon framed in silver above an end table that's actually a half-moon shape.

"Why all the moons?"

Violet frowns, her eyes quickly flitting over every detail. "You said she was dating a vampire?"

"Miss Price, there's no such thing as fucking vampires."

She nods. "Look, there may not be in our world—in the practical world we both inhabit—but in hers? There are. And it's noteworthy."

I give her this and don't argue again.

After scouring Skylar's room and the rest of the apartment, I get directions for Bubbles and Broomsticks. Back in the truck, Violet frowns as she fiddles with Skylar's phone. She's tried her birthday, her astrological sign, every obvious password she could think of, and finally locks herself out of it for fifteen minutes.

"Damn it," she mutters, scowling. She takes her own phone out. "Have you noticed that your sister's companions are all sort of outcasts? You've got Lottie, who's sweet but wears glasses, is overweight and dresses in costumes. Probably not the most popular girl in her class. Were all her friends sort of unpopular?"

"Mhm."

I flick on the directionals and take a left.

"Like… the boyfriend who's essentially androgynous, and I bet if we investigated her other friends, we'd find something similar."

I nod, not sure how this has anything to do with the case.

"Our goal right now is to bring back everything we can to my men. Tonight, we'll go over every detail and see what we can piece together."

"Your men. That sounds so…" Her voice trails off.

"So what?"

"Like, masculine."

I grunt. "What should I call them? My employees?"

She shrugs and gets a little haughty. "It's just that they're not all men anymore."

I look at her full breasts, her petite little body, and those pursed lips I want to kiss. "They're definitely not."

I pull up onto the highway, twenty minutes out from the restaurant we need to investigate. A car whizzes past us so closely, Violet screams. It hits my left tire, ricochets forward, and I have to slam on my brakes to keep it steady.

Violet gasps. "What was that?" I'm already accelerating, following the small black Mazda.

"Are you road raging after them?"

"Me? Road rage? What makes you think I have road rage?"

I'll fucking kill them.

"That was not an accident," Violet says. She's sitting straight up next to me, hands on the dash. "They so did that on purpose."

I'm gaining on them, as they take a sharp right and exit the highway.

"Uh yeah, no reason," she says with a grimace as I follow them off the highway. Horns blare as the light turns red and I plow through it, gaining on them. Someone flips me the bird. The truck's too big to chase them too closely.

"Get the plate," I tell her.

"On it."

The car zigzags in and out of traffic, way too quickly for my huge truck to follow them. I curse under my breath.

"This is not a good getaway car," she mutters.

"No, but it off-roads like a motherfucker and there isn't a better place to be when the shit hits the fan." The glass is shatterproof, the wheels reinforced and nearly invincible. I could mow down a goddamn semi if I had to.

"You can't chase them now, though." She mumbles something under her breath.

"What was that?"

"I said, 'thank God,'" she says loudly. "Not sure what you'd do to them in your present state of mind."

"You work for me now. That means accepting anything and everything that working with me entails. Under any and all circumstances. Understood?"

She nods. "Yes, of course. Why do you think they would hit us?"

"Isn't it obvious?"

"It is, but I want your take. No stone unturned and all that."

"They hit us because they have something to hide. They don't want us on this case. It was a stupid, pussy threat."

I hate that someone basically assaulted us and got away with it.

I call Joe. "Run this plate." I repeat the plate number Violet gives me.

We're going to get answers, and we're going to get them now.

CHAPTER 6

Violet

Something's definitely not right here, I know it in my gut. My mind wanders to the flowers squished against my breast, the phone and cats left unattended in Skylar's room, and the little car that just tried to run us off the road.

"Please tell me the truth," I say to Cain. "Is it more likely that someone has a beef with Skylar or with *you?*"

He clenches his jaw. "Me."

"Thought so. And do you think there's a chance they'd come after her to get back at you?"

He curses again. "Yeah."

I pull up my phone to Google some facts when I remember something. "It's a full moon tonight."

"And?"

I remember Skylar's fascination with moons. I take her phone and type in *full moon.* Nothing.

"Can you name the phases of the moon?"

He gives me a quizzical look, but nods. "Full moon. Waxing crescent. Waning crescent. Waning gibbous… waxing gibbous…" He strokes his chin, a surprisingly masculine move that makes me look away because he's my boss—*correction, no he is not, we work professionally with each other*—and I will not look at how sexy those fingers are rasping against the stubble on his jaw *goddammit.*

I type *waxing crescent.* Nothing. With a sigh, convinced this isn't going to work, I type in *waning crescent.*

Her phone unlocks. I pump the air.

"Got into her phone."

The streets are quiet, the oppressive heat and humidity of late August making the air around us shimmer with haze. Cain guns the engine, as if reminding the universe that he's coming for his sister. "Good work."

I suspect it isn't often that he commends someone who works for him, and his praise sends a warm flicker of pleasure through me. I ignore it. I don't like that I want his praise.

I focus on scrolling through her phone for some clues. I'm violating her privacy, I know I am, but we have to find something that can help us. If we let the police department take their time, it could be too late. I feel sick.

"So, your sister only has like twenty contacts."

"And?"

"Well, it's pretty unusual. The average person has… I don't know, I'd guess hundreds. Huh." I shrug. "That'll make it easier to go through."

"Okay, good."

"But… well, that's not a lot. Is she sort of a loner?"

"Yeah, you could say that."

Bingo. I read a text on her screen that pings my attention.

"She has a text from a guy she's named 'Cowboy.'"

"Cowboy." He frowns. "That's not usually her scene."

It's definitely not.

"Yep."

I flip through the phone. "They met… a week ago… online. He asked her out for drinks and they agreed to go out last night." I don't say anything for a minute, because I'm not sure he wants to hear what's going on in these texts.

"Oh. Oh wow. Then there's a text here, she says, *Don't call me back. I don't ever want to hear from you again.*"

"I want his address."

With the tone he uses, he could replace what he said with *give me the coordinates so I can bomb his ass*.

"And then it looks like there might've been more communication between them, but maybe it was a phone call or several because there are no more texts."

"And there's nothing else?"

I sigh. "I don't see much of anything. She's got some social media stuff... but even that…. Well, there's just Wiccan stuff."

I don't tell him what. He's obviously not a fan of her lifestyle, and I don't know how much is relevant anyway. I scroll through text after text, and it makes me feel shitty. I don't like invading her privacy like this.

But I share his concern. She's in danger, and we need to find her. I look for something, anything at all that will clue me in.

On a whim, I pull up a browser and scroll through her history. Now this is starting to feel more invasive. I ignore the growing unease.

My cheeks scald at the first dozen or so searches.

Doggy style

Reverse 69

Best tantric sex moves

Cowboy

"You're blushing, Miss Price," he says, as he flicks on the directionals and gets off the highway.

"She, uh... not sure how much you want to know. Let's just say I think I know why she calls him Cowboy."

His jaw firms. "Fuck."

"There are maybe some things you don't need to know about your sister."

With a grimace, he shakes his head. "Everything. I need everything."

"She... had a pretty rich sex life, it seems."

He looks like he's just bitten into a lemon. A rotten, mold-covered lemon.

"Sorry."

"Don't be."

I scroll a little more.

"Oh. Oh, wow."

"*What*? Will you please stop that?"

Fuck, I need to find a better poker face.

I shake my head. I will not tell him I had no idea *that* was a position one could put themselves in. I mean, honestly... someone would have to have... like a really, *really* big... in order to fit that way...

"We aren't going to work together if you're hiding things from me."

"I just don't know if you want to know what I'm seeing over here about sexual positions, Mr. Master."

He clamps his mouth shut.

"Some of these are—" I stop talking, as a cold shiver runs down my spine.

Baby's breath.

She has six search histories involving baby's breath and three more with purple irises.

Why?

He pulls into a parking spot outside the restaurant. I remind myself to tell him about the flower search history later.

I need to call my bestie Candi but have to find a way to do it without him knowing, since he doesn't want to involve the police.

I pull out my phone and shoot her a text.

Babe, off record. You were telling me something last night about a recent string of sexual assault victims... what can you tell me about it?

No response. I tuck my phone in my left pocket and Skylar's in my right. He parks the car. I pull up my pants leg to make sure my knife's secured, inwardly groaning when I see the purplish bruises along my shins from getting into his truck. I look like I fell off my bike when my mom took my training wheels off. *Great.*

I don't miss the way people look at us, and I don't think it has anything to do with my odd choice in attire. I can tell that people recognize him, and those that don't, notice him from afar. He's large and intimidating, but that isn't what garners attention so much as the way he walks.

Some people walk like they know you're watching them. Others walk timidly, as if they don't want to step on toes or offend you. Cain walks into the restaurant as if he belongs here and anyone who doesn't ought to fuck off before he makes them. His confident gait and the take-no-prisoners steel in his eyes are silent declarations that he isn't afraid, that if anyone does something dangerous, they'll deal with him. He drips arrogance and violence through his goddamn pores, something that should turn me off.

It doesn't. It doesn't at all.

A few women vaping to the right of the entrance look him up and down, and one even hands her bag to her friend and steps toward us. She gives me a quick look and easily dismisses me as someone who isn't competition, because she doesn't even bother to hide the fact that she likes him, thinks he's hot, and wants to sleep with him, probably right this very minute.

Without missing a beat, Cain slides his large, warm hand along my lower back, curves his fingers around my side and pulls me to him. His eyes are glacial, a man on a mission, but my body doesn't seem to care. At the feel of his hand on me, my blood heats, an electric current coursing its way straight through me. I can't help but step closer to him. I like the way my body tingles, as if every nerve knows this is a man who knows how to treat a woman's body.

The woman heading toward us halts mid-step, then shoots me a scowl. I don't know if I want to stick my tongue out at her or punch her.

We step further inside, and a waitress hands us some menus.

"Do you still have wings on the menu? Babe, you remember those wings you like?"

Babe? Wait, what? Cain Master's just staked his claim on me, and I have no idea why. But when the woman who'd been heading toward us steps to the side, it's starting to become clearer.

I draw in a shaky breath and laugh. I could get into this. "I do. You're the best, honey." *Gag. Me.*

A glimmer of a smile crosses his lips, like a particle of sun breaking through clouds before they swallow it up again. "Anything for you."

This is a front. Nothing more, nothing less.

"Let's sit at the bar," I suggest, gesturing toward the bar.

"Sure thing, baby."

God! He's really pushing this. I make gagging motions with my finger down my throat, then slice my hand in the air in front of me. *Stop!*

He mouths, "*Nope.*"

Argh!

I hop up on a bar stool, but he shakes his head at me. "Scoot over."

"You wanna sit here?"

"I do," he says through tight lips. He's the boss, and he has his reasons, so I move to the left and let him take the seat I was in. "I can see all exits this way."

I'd be pleased if I felt he'd made this move to protect me, but I don't romanticize shit.

The bartender, a thin, kinda young ginger with a scraggly beard and piercings all along each ear and his eyebrow welcomes us. "Can I get you two a drink?"

His eyes linger a little longer on Cain. He recognizes him, I think. Hard to forget a guy like him.

"Soda water with lemon," I order. Cain gets a soda.

"I know you," the bartender says to Cain when he hands us our drinks. Bingo.

"Yeah?" Cain takes a sip of his drink and places it back on the counter. His eyes flit over my shoulder, scanning the entrance, before he looks back at the bartender. He folds his arms across his chest, and his muscles bulge. I don't know if he's trying to intimidate him on purpose, but the bartender takes a step back. "How do you know me?"

"On second thought, not sure I do. You remind me of someone."

He turns to walk away.

"He's Skylar's brother," I say loudly enough to get his attention. "Do you know her?" I keep a close eye on the people watching us. Does anyone look guilty? Curious? Does anyone know her?

Cain shoots his eyes to me, the quickest glance. I pull out my phone and open up a picture of her.

"We're actually looking for her," I say casually. "Have you seen her recently?"

The bartender wipes down condensation from my glass, then slides it over to me as my phone beeps. "Haven't seen her."

He doesn't make eye contact, though, and as soon as someone else comes to the bar, he walks away from us to take their order.

"He's lying and avoiding us." I sip my soda and check my phone.

"Agreed. The question is, why?"

There's a string of texts from Candi.

Candi: Where are you? No one's seen you at work and you never miss.

Me: I'm doing a job. I can't tell you any more right now.

Candi: Are you safe?

I look at Cain. Am I safe? Hell no, I'm not safe. But he's likely not going to hurt me in the next few minutes, so I can lie for now. I have to.

Me: Yes.

Candi: What did you need to know?

Me: You said there was a rise in sexual assault cases lately. What did you tell me about flowers?

Candi: It's his signature move. He leaves flowers for his victims before he rapes them. Why do you need to know?

I don't reply.

The baby's breath at my breast feels suddenly hot, burning against my skin like a brand.

I try to reason with myself. Not every flower is a sign.

I'm going crazy.

Half a minute later, another text comes in.

Candi: Hey. You're nowhere to be found then the next thing I know, you're asking me about active cases. Way to freak me out. What the hell is going on?

Me: I don't know. I glance at the monster of a man sitting beside me and release a breath. *I'm safe. That's all I can tell you right now. Have there been any survivors?*

Candi: Two

Shit. *Fuck.*

I have some research to do tonight.

Cain's scowling at his phone, too.

"Anything important?"

"Yeah. They got the details on the car that hit us, but the car was stolen so there's no way to tell who was driving."

"And the lights?"

"Someone reconfigured the timing grid at the intersection."

Also notable.

I have to find out more about the missing women and the surviving victims. I open my phone again, and I Google shit I *never want to Google* until I've got a list of details involving the rape crimes around here lately. I do not tell any of this to Cain quite yet, because I have to find a way to do it without giving him a coronary.

I make notes on my phone.

Tonight, I'll look up every detail I can until I have a better idea of what's going on.

I slug the rest of my drink and raise my hand for another, just so I can get the bartender to come over.

He glances from me to Cain apprehensively. "Need a refill?"

He nods.

I watch as the bartender fills both of our glasses. He jerks his head behind him. "Be right there."

He's just trying to get us to not ask questions, I know he is, because I see no one has called him, no one who's waiting for him.

I turn on my most charming smile. "Oh, hey," I say, crooking my finger at him to stay before he goes off again. "I actually have a few more pictures of the girl we're looking for." I try to keep my tone casual, my body language relaxed. I wish I could send a message to Cain to lighten the hell up, because he's definitely not contributing to the casual, relaxed vibe I'm going for here.

The look the bartender shoots Cain is nothing short of terrified, but I talk quickly so he doesn't look at Cain and looks at me instead. "I've got a few more pictures for you." I pull up the pictures I swiped from Skylar's social media. "It's really, really important we find her. Are you sure you didn't see her? She was here last night on a date."

The bartender rubs a hand across his face. I read once that touching one's face is a classic sign of guilt or nerves, and I note this carefully. My guess is he didn't have a direct hand in taking her, but somehow helped the people who did or at least knows who they are.

Son of a bitch.

I glance at Cain, narrowing my eyes to tell him to stop looking like the Grim Reaper, then quickly glance at the bartender.

Cain leans forward on his big, beefy arms, his voice a low drawl. "I'd be very pleased if you could help us find her. Like she said, she's my sister." *Implication: And I'll be pissed if you don't.*

"Right." The bartender's words are barely above a whisper.

Cain flashes a disarming grin that somehow makes my nerves stand on edge. There's something about that smile I don't trust. There isn't an ounce of humor in his body right now. "I'm not sure we've met before?"

He extends his large hand out. It's then that I notice small tattoos along the inner side of one hand. I can't see what they are yet, but there's a lot of them.

"Name's Cain Master."

Now this time, there's nothing left to the imagination. The bartender pales, and only after prompting from Cain, reaches out and gingerly takes his hand. "I've heard a lot about you, sir."

Cain shrugs. "Eh, people like to embellish facts. I bet half of what you heard isn't true."

And the other half is.

The bartender doesn't reply at first. Then he clears his throat, and when he speaks, it's in a low whisper. "Meet me by the dumpster out back. We can't talk here."

Cain slowly picks up his drink and sips. I take inventory. There's one more bartender near the dishwasher, unloading clean, steaming hot glasses and placing them on a rack. A few people glance our way, but most are drinking or dancing, and in one corner of the room, some people play pool. A waitress sidles past me with a tray of pizza that looks so good my mouth waters.

Damn, this place is teeming with people, from young adults to teens, and I'm starving. I haven't eaten in way too long.

"Finish your drink," Cain says in a low whisper. "Then follow me."

The bartender wipes down the space in front of him, turns, and leaves. He walks down a hall that leads to a door, a broken *restroom* sign leading his way. The door shuts behind him.

A minute later, Cain gets up from his seat, tosses a few bills on the bar for the tab, then goes out the door the way the bartender went. I follow. Someone crosses in front of me, putting more distance between me and the guys.

Before I can reach them, an alarm goes off. White lights flash. The wail of a siren goes off and sprinklers water down on us.

"Everyone evacuate!" someone shouts, just as the smell of acrid smoke reaches me.

Utter chaos erupts.

You don't realize how crowded a place is until you all try to evacuate at once. One minute ago, the place was relatively calm, save some voices and laughter. Now, it's a zoo.

People shove past me. Some scream, and others have the rabid look of someone being chased. I might be small, but I won't let myself get trampled. Someone in front of me shoves me back. I throw my shoulder, knocking them down.

"Hey!" her boyfriend says, and the dumbass thinks he's somehow entitled to hit me. I duck his hand, and in one quick movement, sweep his leg. With the crowd pushing on him, it's the most effective way to make sure he stays down. His girlfriend screams. I take the opportunity to run.

I'm small, so it's easy to dodge the melee of people around me. I wonder where Cain is, but I'm not too worried. Something tells me he can take care of himself.

I get to the exit when someone grabs me from behind. I feel strong fingers at the nape of my neck. On instinct, my hand flies up to block the touch just before I bend and strike at the torso behind the grasp.

I gasp when I see Cain doubled over, the people around us swarming past, oblivious to us. Shit! Sirens scream, coming closer.

"Fuck," he pants, still doubled over. "It was a set-up. And Jesus, look before you fucking strike. Come with me."

It's then that I realize there's blood dripping down his forehead and a gash on his upper left arm, and neither one of those were because of my self-defense moves.

"Are you alright?"

"I'm fine. Follow me." He sidesteps people left and right, then ducks down behind a barrel. He tugs me down beside him. Fire trucks come down the street, their sirens piercing the air. Our hiding space is so small, I'm right up against him, my back against his thighs. I keep myself very, very still.

His voice is a low vibration in my ear. "Stay here. We're waiting until this has all died down. He pulled the fucking alarm trigger thinking it would scare us off."

"Asshole. I don't scare off that easily."

"Good," he says from behind me. His voice is a low rumble, his warm breath on my neck. "I don't either. And now, we wait. The son of a bitch set me up."

I would *not* want to be that bartender right about now.

"How do you know it was a setup?"

"The second I stepped outside of the bar, he was gone, the alarm went off, and when people poured out of the bar, I was attacked."

I suspected he knew something. This only confirms it.

"Who attacked you?"

"Couldn't see. Someone hooded, and they took off the second the place evacuated."

"Son of a bitch." I wobble in my crouched position, and without a word, he wraps his hand around my waist to steady me. His hand's large enough that his grip on one side rights my whole body. My skin seems to flame beneath the heat of his touch. I force myself to stay focused.

The firefighters come, finish evacuating the place, and put out a small kitchen fire. I look in every direction to see where the bartender might have hidden. I pull up the bar website and look for everything I can find. They have a profile page with the name of everyone who works here. I get to work.

By the time the crowd's dissipated, I've got everything I need to know about the bartender.

"You think they think we're gone?"

"Long gone."

"Good."

We wait for what seems like hours. I don't move. I barely even breathe. We're safe in our hiding place, but our location could be revealed at any moment, so I stay exactly where I am. His hand's still on me, steadying me. My breathing's ragged and unsteady.

I blink in surprise when I see the bartender. I hiss to Cain, "I saw him. He went in just now through the back door to the stock room. Plan of attack?"

He grunts. "I'll go in first. I'll—"

"Let me go in first. I'm smaller and it will be easier for me to find him."

"Absolutely not, and do not interrupt me again."

I stifle a whine. *Of course not. Yes, sir! ::inward eye roll::*

His voice rings with authority. "I'll find him. I'll question him. You'll do what I tell you."

I grumble at him, "Take notes on my notepad and maybe make you a sandwich?"

The grip on my waist, which I *almost* forgot about, tightens. "Careful, Miss Price. Don't push it."

Now why would I do a thing like that? *Grrr!*

I see a glimmer of red hair through a window.

"He's definitely there."

"Where?"

"Ten o'clock, behind the door, but close enough to a window if you need that entrance as well." Ha, who am I kidding? The only one of us who'd fit through a window is me. He'd be lucky to get a leg through.

I hear the unmistakable sound of a gun being cocked. "Let's go."

Seconds later, we move as one, crouched but running to the back entrance of the restaurant. I test the handle and find it locked. Silently, Cain jerks his head for me to get out of the way and pulls a small, slender device out of his pocket. He slides it expertly in place. The lock clicks, and the door swings open.

Cain goes in first. Prepared for an ambush, I don't look. This is not going to end well. The ginger bartender looks at us, turns, and tries to run away. In one swift move, I take my knife out of the ankle harness, aim, and fling it through the air. It lands like an arrow, the blade sunk deep into the wood of the doorframe half an inch from his head.

"Stay right there."

CHAPTER 7

Cain

I KNEW she was skilled with a knife, but the way she stopped him mid-stride was fucking beautiful. So graceful, it fucking made me hard. Her skill goes way beyond beginner.

I don't waste time. In three firms strides across the room I've got the bartender by the neck.

"Name."

"Jeremy Guard."

"Why the fuck did you try to get rid of me?"

His eyes water and his voice squeaks, like a cornered mouse.

"Because they'll kill me."

"Who will?"

"I don't know names."

"Are they the people that took my sister?"

"I—I think so."

I grip his shirt and shake him.

"Yes!"

"Where are they?"

"I don't know. Said something about heading to Canada, but I can't tell you anything beyond that."

Fucking Canada?

"Why will they kill you?"

"Because they don't want to get caught. Because they'd go to jail for life. Because it would end their little shopping spree." He's crying freely now.

How fucking dare he. I give him another shake, furious he had the nerve to call it a *shopping spree*.

"That's my sister we're talking about."

Jeremy nods.

"Give me one fucking reason why *I* shouldn't kill you."

"Because I'm your ticket to finding them."

Wily son of a bitch.

"Yeah? You have no names. You've got no connections. How do I know what you've said is true?"

"Because they come all the time. They'll be back."

"And what's your role in this?"

He closes his eyes and winces. I shake him again, but Violet is so over this. She gives him a swift kick to the calf. "He asked you a question!"

He flinches and cries out. She glares at him, beautiful and feisty but ferocious as hell. Christ, even I'd answer her question. I did the right thing hiring her.

"They paid me! And I need the money."

A deadly calm comes over me. My gun burns on my hip, ready to dance in my grip and make him pay. "Why?"

"I owe a bookie," he sobs. "I didn't want to do it."

"Do *what*?"

He doesn't answer but closes his eyes and cries harder, like he knows his honest answer will sign his death warrant.

"You tell me, or I'll hold you down and give her permission to beat you. Is that what you want? To be beaten by a woman?"

He winces. Violet assumes a fighting stance, fucking ready.

Gorgeous.

He shakes his head. "He paid me to... slip them roofies."

Motherfucker. The date rape drug.

The hand holding him in my grip shakes with fury. "Then what?"

"Then he'd… pick them up. Take them home. And I don't know what from there. I try to respect people who—"

"Oh, fuck *off.*"

He stares at the gun in my hand.

I don't give him a chance to explain further. He starts to cry. "I never meant to hurt anyone."

I grab him by the hair and shove him to his knees. If I had time, I'd torture the motherfucker. I want to see the same pain in his eyes the women he fed to the goddamn wolves felt. I want to hear him cry harder and beg for his life until he's hoarse.

"You fucking piece of shit." My voice shakes and the room blurs. "If my sister's with a rapist right now… if he hurts her… it's your fucking fault."

I knee him, and when he doubles over, I hammer my fist to his jaw. Bone snaps, blood spurts. Violet watches in approval and cracks her knuckles like she wants to help me.

"You're a worthless, spineless bastard. Any man that helps another take advantage of innocent women deserves punishment worse than death." I grab him by the hair and yank his head back. I want to slit his throat. I want to feel his warm blood spill on my own hands as his life seeps out of him. I want to watch his eyes grow lifeless.

I have to get to Skylar. And Violet's watching.

I hit him again, and again, until he's whimpering and bloodied, his eyes swollen shut.

"Cain," Violet whispers. "We have to go. He deserves this. He deserves to be tortured and raped just like those girls he helped hurt. But we have to get Skylar."

"This asshole slipped roofies to unsuspecting women. He helped a known rapist who now might have my fucking sister."

I don't think about the choices. Out of time, I pull my gun and slide the silencer on. I ignore his pleas, the way he cries like a baby and begs for mercy. I put the gun to his temple.

"You'll never hurt another innocent woman."

"No! God, no, please," he says through blood and spittle. The hand holding my gun shakes.

"You can look away, Miss Price."

"No."

I pull the trigger.

Violet watches with a slight frown as his body hits the floor, blood splashing on the floor beside her. She kneels and takes his pulse.

"You're right. He won't."

I call Joe.

"429 Might Street. Team alpha."

"Five minutes out, sir."

I hang up the phone and look at Violet. She doesn't look upset, as I expected her to. She doesn't even look disturbed. Her lips are a thin line, and something like triumph lights her beautiful, vivid eyes so they sparkle like amethyst.

That should warn me. Sane people don't watch someone being executed and rejoice in their death. But I don't feel anything but a sort of camaraderie.

"I'm sorry you had to see that."

She gives one short shake of her head. "Don't be. I'm sorry his death was so quick." She stands in silent acceptance that I just killed a man. We both know it's only a prelude to what I'll do when I find who he was helping.

We don't talk. We barely look at each other.

There was a time when I could still remember the names and faces of the people I'd killed.

That was a long time ago.

In exactly three minutes, our team has arrived to take care of the details.

I jerk my chin at her. "Let's go."

This time, she walks with me of her own accord and there's no need to threaten her.

"You didn't hesitate."

"Hesitate?"

"To kill him." Her voice is a bit strained, but she looks otherwise normal.

"No. Why would I?"

She shrugs. "You just... you didn't second-guess."

"No."

"You shot him because he deserved it, and you have no regrets."

I don't even think about my answer before I speak. "Yes."

"If I ask you an honest question..."

"You'll get an honest answer."

A beat passes before she tips her head to the side and asks, "Do these pants make me look fat?"

I stifle a snort. "How can you make jokes at a time like this?" I can't help the corners of my lips from turning upward.

"You'll see I'm surprisingly skilled at comic relief during the absolute *worst* times. It's one of my skills I should've mentioned during our interview."

The door to the room shuts fast behind us, hiding our team and the body they'll dispose of.

Our boots stomp heavily on the concrete toward my truck.

"I'll look forward to it."

She releases a shuddering breath. I look at her sharply. Good God, she's not going to start... *crying.* Is she?

But no. When she catches me looking at her, her eyes are dry and her lips are in a thin, firm line. "I pulled up everything I could on our little friend."

"The one we left with our other friends?"

"The very same."

"Tell me in the truck. Someone helped him, and I'm not sure who, but we aren't safe here."

She steps up the pace, and I move closer to her. When we reach the truck, I don't wait for her to fight her way up and bang the hell out of her shins again. She thinks I didn't see that. I remember the feel of her against me when I pinned her to the ground, and the feel of her body pressed to mine while we crouched in wait. I want to feel her again.

Before she has a chance to react, I reach for her and lift her up as easily as if she were a child. Her feet scissor and she gives a little squeak, but I don't wait around for the inevitable lecture or eye roll. I plop her down safely and walk to my side.

As soon as I open my door, she starts in.

"Excuse me," she says sternly, before I get the door to the truck closed shut.

"I know, don't touch you, don't help you, let you bruise the shit out of your shins. No." I crank the engine and look through my rearview mirrors, not an easy feat considering they fucked my mirrors up.

"Why? How? Seriously, how do you justify being such a control freak?"

"Me? Control freak?" I laugh quietly to myself, and mutter, "You have no idea." I would enjoy the ever-living hell out of having some modicum of control over her.

Dusk has settled on the city, the bluish haze of late summer making everything look mysterious and ethereal. I drive toward the road that takes me home, glancing in the rearview mirror so many times I'm barely watching where I'm going on the main road.

She's typing away on her phone, muttering to herself, taking notes, when she looks out the window and stares.

"Thinking?"

She doesn't reply for long minutes, just picks at a cuticle on one hand. "What do they do with the body?"

This would be a shitty time for her to start crying about all this.

"Better if you don't know, but it won't be a problem." A beat passes.

"Take me home now, please. I've never needed a shower more in my life."

I don't want to take her home. I want to keep her with me until we find Skylar. But I know we have research to do, and my team is on it. We have to find the person who hit us today and follow up on the contacts on Skylar's phone, along with whoever else at the bar's connected to the disappearances. And I'll be worth shit if I don't get some sleep.

"I'll take you home, and you do all the research you can. Tomorrow, we meet with my team to compare what we've found and hopefully make moves. Remember what I said about packing a bag."

"Right."

Tugging down her top, she moves her bra to the side and pulls out the sprig of delicate white flowers. I swivel my eyes back to the road so I don't confirm how the little sprig of flowers left an imprint on her bare breasts. I shift uncomfortably in the driver's seat, trying to rein in my focus. She has small, perfect breasts that would fit—

Christ.

"We need to keep this in mind. Whoever's taking them leaves flowers for them before he goes. One of those signature moves? There were flowers on the walkway to your sister's house, and your sister was looking for the meaning of them. I found it in the search history of her phone."

Shit.

"We don't really have the luxury of assuming anything's a coincidence right now."

We don't.

She's quiet, looking out the window. Holding something back from me.

"What is it?"

"It's just... well, there were flowers at work. I teach kickboxing classes to little kids, and before I left the other night, I saw some. It's probably not related, though."

"Is your studio near a florist or a delivery shop or a supermarket that might sell flowers?"

"No."

"Fuck going home," I tell her, as I turn to take the entrance to the highway. "You'll come back to my place." To my home, the goddamn fortress, where I've got my own army of trained soldiers who aren't afraid of combat.

She draws in a breath then releases it slowly, but she doesn't respond at first.

"I'm not giving you a choice in this. I'm—"

"Giving me a choice or I walk." I feel my brows snap together, but before I can respond, she continues. "I appreciate your concern. But I'm fully capable of taking care of myself."

"I thought we already had this discussion this morning, and that conversation ended with me on top of you."

Her hands clench into fists, but I don't fucking care. My sister's with God-knows-who, I've got no leads whatsoever on whatever the fuck is going on, I just put a bullet through a man's skull, and now she thinks she has a choice in this.

"You may have noticed, Miss Price, that my entire staff resides at my house."

"I have." She frowns in a way that looks almost like a pout. "It's odd and borderline cultish."

I won't let her get a rise out of me.

"I have my reasons. Scattering my employees and the contractors that work for me would be a terrible decision, as my necessary resources would be dispersed and weakened. I provide ample accommodations and security."

"Right. But what you may not have noticed is that the only female in your residence is an elderly, likely married woman."

"And the doctor."

"Oh wow. You hired a female doctor? How modern of you."

There's a low rumble in the truck I don't realize is my own damn growl at first.

"I'm not offering for you to live with me, Miss Price." I huff out a humorless laugh. "Don't flatter yourself."

She mutters something under her breath.

"What's that?"

She doesn't respond.

Her stomach growls, loud and clear. Now that I understand. "You're hungry. At least come and get something to eat before you go home."

"I'm good, thanks. I've got plenty of food at my house."

"Are you hungry or not?"

"Starving, but legitimate hunger's good for the soul. I'll somehow make it this time."

Stubborn. So goddamn stubborn. I don't miss the way she sits as far away from me as she can, as if somehow forming a physical distance will keep her safe.

I try another tactic. "I prefer the people that work for me to be safe. You don't have reliable transportation or a way to get anywhere if I need you right away. You were the one that picked up on details today we need to pursue, and I want you to report to my team directly so we can pool our resources. If anyone or anything hurts you, our entire operation is at risk."

She nods, slowly. "I see. But still, no."

Maddening woman! I clench my teeth and force myself to speak calmly. "And what will you do if someone attacks you?"

She's quiet for a minute, then finally shrugs. "You're not the only one with weapons, Mr. Master."

This woman's full of surprises.

"Fine. I'll take you home. Pack a bag so you're ready for the next time we work together. I'll send one of the company cars to your house for your use."

"Thank you." Finally, something she doesn't argue with.

She gives me her address, and we drive the rest of the way to her home in silence.

"You're brooding."

"I'm not brooding." Jesus, I haven't met anyone in years who's so goddamn free with me. Does she have zero sense of self-preservation? We don't speak again for long minutes, as the houses and cars pass by our windows, dimly lit in the moonlight. Streetlamps cast shadows on the street and sidewalks.

When we're a block away, she turns to me.

"I'm sorry about your sister. Tonight, I'm going to look up anything and everything I can. I'll make a list of notes and leads, and come over tomorrow to help you continue the investigation. And if anything happens while I'm gone, please let me know."

"I will. Look up everything you can about the flowers and the cases they suspect are linked."

"I will."

"You should get some sleep, though."

"So should you."

We both know neither one of us will sleep tonight.

I hate that my sister's out there. I hate that we have so little to go on.

It's easier to handle cases that don't involve the people you love.

And I hate that Violet's going home.

CHAPTER 8

Violet

It seems like I've lived a dozen lives this week, and I'm weary. So tired, my bones feel like they creak, and my eyelids feel paper thin. I want to crawl in my bed, face first, right on top of the blankets and not get up again for a good, long while.

I left here this morning wanting to get hired by Cain Master.

I got a lot more than I bargained for.

His huge, ambling truck pulls out in front of my place. My landlord Troy's smoking a butt on the top stoop, and he doesn't even bother to try to hide the fact that he's scoping out Cain and his truck. I watch him take a drag, then let the smoke out slowly. He tosses it to the next step down and grinds it under his heel before he starts to come our way.

Seriously?

"Who's this?" Cain murmurs, his voice deceptively casual.

"Landlord. Usually just keeps to himself. This is weird."

"He got a thing for you?"

I can't help but snort at that. "Uh, no." No one's got a "thing" for me, but I don't think Cain believes me. Troy anchors his hands on his hips and glares at us.

"Come at me, bro," Cain says quietly.

"Okay, relax," I say with an eye roll. "He is *not* worth your time. Trust me. I can handle him."

"That was never in question," he mutters, releasing the wheel and cracking his neck, like he's limbering up for a fight. Maybe he wants someone to pick a fight with him, to help burn off the intensity of the aggression that rolls off him. Maybe he wants to kick some ass.

Shiver.

"Alright, fine. I'll have a car brought here within the hour, and I want you at my place at eight a.m. sharp tomorrow morning."

Well then. Someone likes to gain back control. Well played, Mr. Master.

I'll play along right back.

"Of course. And thank you."

"Don't forget to pack your clothes."

I bite down some snarky remarks and turn away from him so he doesn't see my eye roll.

"Yessiree," I mutter, as I swing my legs around toward my side of the truck. The clouds shift, and a stream of moonlight hits the ground beside it. I look up at the full, brilliant white moon, and a pang hits my heart. *Skylar.* Where is she? What's happening to her? Is she okay?

And she isn't even my sister. I can't begin to imagine what he's going through. He's learned how to school his features, how to hide his feelings. Years of service and what he's been through would do that to a person.

We'll find her.

I push open the truck door. Cain opens his mouth to say something, but I don't give him a chance.

"Thank you for everything," I say loudly, infusing a lilt of flirtation in my voice, as if he just brought me home after homecoming, for Troy's benefit. *Cringe.* "I'll see you in the morning."

He gives me a little finger wave but doesn't reply. He's focused instead on watching Troy.

"If this fucker gives you any trouble…" he begins in a low rumble.

"Kick him where the sun don't shine. On it." To be more accurate, I'd curse him out and call Candi, since I typically try not to get into any altercations with my landlord. I did that once, and things got a bit... messy. It's hard to find a new apartment mid-month.

I step down from the truck, and Cain yells from behind me, "Call me before you go to bed, baby!"

God. He's doing that fake boyfriend thing again. I shoot him a glare over my shoulder, but that only makes him do this deep, manly, sexy chuckle I feel straight between my legs. *Grrr!*

Troy stares. What the hell is his problem? "Tell your boyfriend he can't park there," he says, but once he catches sight of Cain, he starts to take a step backward. Smart move, asshole.

It's on the tip of my tongue to tell him he's not my boyfriend, but I think better of it. It might be good for word to get around I've got a boyfriend the size of Paul Bunyan, who drives a truck the size of Paul's big blue ox. I amuse myself with the memory of the fabled Paul Bunyan rolling over in his sleep and causing an earthquake, and digging out the Great Lakes by hand.

I fantasized about being friends with Paul Bunyan when I was a little girl, bullied by my foster parents and bullied at school. No one would bully a girl with a friend who was bigger than life.

I guess I never outgrew that.

As Cain's truck drives away, I square my shoulders and head inside.

I walk up the steps and grab my mail, and for once in my life my landlord doesn't give me shit or follow me. Thank you, Mr. Master. I did tell him I don't need help, and I don't, but I might as well take advantage when opportunity knocks.

Now that the sun has set, it's cooler, and even the humidity's lessened. My phone beeps. I look down to see a text from Candi.

Candi: Just checking to see if you're still alive.

Me: I will be more alive after I get some food in my belly.

I'm so starving, my vision's blurred. I walk up the flight of stairs, open my apartment door, then shut it and deadbolt it behind me. I breathe a sigh of relief that I've somehow made it this far. We do breathing exercises when we train, and it comes naturally to me when I feel the tension along my neck and back.

Deep breath in. Release.

After everything that's happened the past few days, I feel like I need to scope my place out before I relax.

The kitchen looks untouched. Nothing out of place. I left everything locked up tighter than a drum, the windows shut and locked, the air conditioner on low. The kitchen's clear.

The bathroom's got a small, standing shower with a clear glass door, and it's easy to see it's vacant as well. Not a towel or tissue out of place.

I turn to leave the bathroom when a loud crash sounds behind me in my bedroom. I scream, swivel on my heel, and my knife's in my hand before I've stopped screaming. I stand in place, my hand trembling.

"Who's there? Come out! I swear to God, if you don't, I'll kill you!"

I walk into my bedroom. A light breeze flutters through an open window, a curtain dancing in the wind. No one's there.

That's odd. I never leave my window open. Why the hell would I forget this one?

I swing around and look at my closet, but it's wide open and so tiny, no one could fit in there if they tried. There's nowhere else to hide in my rinky-dink apartment.

Why the hell did I think this was a good idea again? *Why?*

Independence is so overrated.

There's a fucking serial rapist on the loose, and the guy I'm working for not only has an enormous kitchen stocked with food I saw with my very own eyes, he has things like security guards and guns. Big ones.

Not the only big thing he's got, I think to myself like a horny teen, but someone's got to break the tension, and I'm the only one here.

"Good one, Vi. Keep 'em rolling," I mutter to myself just to break the silence.

I walk around my room, suddenly angry that anyone's done anything at all to make me afraid, to think they can come into my goddamn house and hurt me. Blood pulses through my veins, boiling.

Come at me. Fight me. If even Cain Master himself took me on now, it would be a battle to the death.

"Who's there? Come out! Come show yourself to me!"

Nothing. Not a sound. I look on the floor as something catches my eye. A picture frame's fallen from my desk. The wind knocked it over, and here I am thinking I have a damn intruder.

I roll my eyes and pick it up. My doorbell buzzes.

Interesting. I go to the living room and push the intercom button, curious. "Yes?"

"Delivery for a Miss Price."

Delivery?

"What is it?"

"Sake and Sushi."

Sake and Sushi's the name of one of my favorite places to eat. "I didn't order Sake and Sushi," I say, even as my stomach growls and my mouth waters. I swallow hard. I *wish* that was my order.

"Delivery ordered from a Master Enterprises, ma'am."

No. He didn't!

"Come up."

I hit the buzzer, and a moment later, look through the peephole to find a delivery guy standing with an enormous takeout bag of food.

I open the door, and he hands me the bag. "Let me tip you—"

"Already been taken care of. Good night."

And off he goes.

The smell wafts through the air, and my knees wobble. I'm weak with hunger.

My phone buzzes with a text.

Cain.

I tap it, and a picture fills my screen. It's a stunning, hefty black SUV with chrome rims that gleam under the streetlights. Oh my God.

Cain: This is your company vehicle. It's been dropped off by your front door and I'm sending you an attachment with a digital key. Once you open it, you'll find the physical key in the glovebox, entry code your birthday. You'll have a gas card as well and unlimited mileage.

Me: Okay, Mr. Master, what's the catch?

No response at first.

Cain: Most people say thank you, Miss Price.

Me: I'm not most people. What goes up must come down and all that.

Cain: The catch is, I still want your ass at my place in the morning for target practice.

Me: And?

Cain: And nothing. I'm assuming you'll do the work I asked you to do tonight, and that's all. Enjoy your dinner.

Me: Thank you.

My hand hovers over the little smiley face emoji, but on second thought I don't send it. I have to stay strong. I can't let him wine and dine me.

Mouth watering, I open the takeout bag to find a small pile of white cardboard boxes. I swallow. Oh my God, there's enough food here for an army. Vegetable tempura, lightly breaded and fried until golden brown, skewers of savory beef and chicken teriyaki, steamed rice with their signature veggies fresh from their rooftop garden, shrimp and rice, delicate rows of spring rolls, and a variety of fresh, decadent sushi, neatly nestled in pretty silver trays.

Candi's got a night shift, and I don't know anyone else close enough to share this with. Ah, well. Breakfast, lunch, and dinner for the next week, and I am *not* complaining.

I eat standing up right at the counter, savoring every decadent morsel.

"My God, food this good should not even be legal," I mutter to myself around a mouthful of shrimp tempura as I open up the laptop and fire it up.

I've got work to do.

I start with the notes on my phone.

When I'm good and stuffed, I package up the leftover food and slide it into my fridge, my mind teeming with the knowledge I've gleaned.

Precisely thirteen victims since June.

God. It's worse than I thought.

Several eyewitnesses insist they saw the same man with a string of victims before they went missing, but things aren't adding up.

"I know it was him," one father said about his daughter's kidnapper. "He fits this exact profile."

Who? The profile fits a man by the name of Derrick Dossier, a former police officer, retired from the force at the age of forty-nine. Some sources even found his DNA at the crime scene and on victims, which normally is strong evidence to convict. But every single time, there was undeniable evidence that Dossier had an ironclad alibi, most with video and photographic evidence. And since humans are unable to bi-locate, he was let off despite overwhelming evidence against him.

I look at my notes, wishing I hadn't eaten that last piece of shrimp. My stomach's in knots.

Anita Charles

Age: 18

Taken August 1, found dead August 4th.

Clear victim of repeated rape. Bruises found along inner thighs and anus, lesions throughout the body.

Note: Sources say she received bouquets left at her door several days before she was taken.

Margaret Sellier

Age: 19

Taken August 5th, found dead August 7th

Raped multiple times. Bruised and subjected to beatings. Broken bones and teeth.

Note: Sources say there were fresh flowers at her residence when she was taken.

Clair Boyd

Age: 18

Taken August 8th. Survivor.

Has no memory of abuse but shows signs of repeated rape and abuse. Trauma amnesia.

Note: No flowers on record

I SPEND the next two hours scrolling through every bit of social media involving the girls that I can, as well as every report I can get my hands on.

Anita left home at the age of sixteen and was estranged from her parents as well as her siblings. She came from a religious home and had nine brothers and sisters. "She left us for the occult," her mother's on record as saying. "I knew things would end like this. I knew she'd be taken by the Devil for her sins."

A lump rises in my throat, reminding me of the minister's wife who rejected me. I don't know how some people live with themselves in the name of something that should be good.

Anita has a mere twelve followers online, and the news said no one came to her funeral.

Strange.

I flip through her pictures, not surprised to see she classifies herself as Wiccan, but has very few friends. There are patterns like the pieces to a puzzle scattered on a table, beginning to take form but still just a jumble of cardboard. I need to fit more pieces into place before I can see the whole picture.

Margaret Sellier has a similar story. Left home at eighteen, got a double associates degree from a local community college. But reports say she was "strange" and "odd." Further investigation shows she was known for resisting mainstream culture, publicly and vocally.

I pace my apartment. Thinking.

If I were someone looking to take advantage of women... I would want to take someone no one would miss. It would cover my tracks if I took someone who might be involved with things their family didn't approve of, so said family might blame their social groups or behavior on their disappearance...

It's after midnight when I close my laptop and go to shower. I strip my clothes off halfway down the hall and toss them into the hamper just before I get to the bathroom. I wish I could cleanse what I've read from my mind, but I'm determined now. I will find the person responsible for these crimes.

A pang of guilt hits me.

I haven't thought about finding my parents' murderers in hours. I haven't gone that long without thinking about them in... God, years.

I tell myself this is only a means to an end. Help him, and he'll help me. I'm only working with him for this one reason, so I can leverage his power and connections.

I put the water on to scalding and glance down at myself. God, I'm a mess. Between the stupid accident and bruising my shins all to hell today on Cain's car, I'm covered in bruises and lacerations and smudges of dirt. How could that guy hit on me?

Did he hit on me?

I stare at myself in the mirror, just before the steam fogs it up entirely. My body may be damaged, but my eyes are the same vivid shade of violet as ever.

I should maybe get those color-changing contacts. If I'm on the hunt for someone, they'll remember a girl with eyes like mine.

I text Cain. I bet he'll be able to get them quicker than I will.

Me: Hey, I know it's late, hopefully you do the 'do not disturb' after a certain hour thing

The response is immediate.

Cain: Everything okay?

Guess he doesn't.

My heart thumps. I probably woke the guy up, and his first question is, am I okay? This is *after* he bought me dinner and *a car*.

And after he tried to boss you around and showed absolutely no respect for your self-respect or autonomy. NO THANK YOU.

Me: I'm fine, but I wondered if you

I pause mid-text, trying to figure out how to word my question just right. My finger is hovering over the phone when my eyes graze the windowsill in my bedroom. I'm on the second floor near the fire escape. The breeze still flutters the curtains at the window, only now the windowsill isn't empty.

A sprig of purple irises sits on the ledge.

CHAPTER 9

Cain

I WATCH the little dots on the screen dance, then stop, dance, then stop. I asked her if she's okay and expected a quick response, probably something snarky.

Fine, just polishing my guns. You?

All good, haven't found any strange men lying in wait or abductees behind my shower curtain, how bout you?

I'm fine, you can call off the babysitters now.

I SENT HER A CAR, but I sent a small team to watch her, too. If she's right about the asshole being after her, I don't want to take any chances.

A minute passes. Two. Three.

No response.

I'm in my bedroom in shorts and a tank after a shower, prepared to do whatever work I can through the night. I've got a team ready to be briefed in the morning and people working around the clock already.

I go to text her, then stop. Then again. Finally, I decide the hell with it, and shoot her another text.

Me: Hey. You were typing and now nothing. Everything alright?

No response.

I pick up my phone and call Henri, the head of the team I sent to her apartment. His phone rings and goes to voicemail.

No response.

I pull on shoes and grab a jacket, slipping it on as I leave my room.

"Everything alright?" Joe asks me when I hit the foyer at a jog. I fill him in.

"You think she's in danger?"

"After today? Not something I wanna risk."

I should've duct taped her to her seat and made her come home with me.

"I'll join you. You taking the Audi?" His eyes gleam, hoping I am.

"Hell yes."

The truck is good for an ambush, for safety, for a potential shoot-out. But when I have to get somewhere *fast*? I take the Audi. It goes from zero to sixty in 2.8 seconds and drives up to two hundred seventeen miles per hour. It's swift, takes corners with agility, but is small and sleek enough not to cause too much attention if I'm careful.

Her apartment is twenty-five minutes away according to GPS. We'll get there in ten.

"What are you packing?" Joe asks. We step into the room we affectionately call the armory, where our weapons are securely and discreetly stored.

"Ruger and a blade. You?"

The Ruger EC9 functions as one of the best compact concealed pistols money can buy, small and sleek but lethal.

"EC9. Which blade?"

"MK3." I take it from its sheath and give it a quick look-over. "Are there any others?" The Ontario MK3's a standard Navy SEAL weapon, six inches of hardened steel perfection finished with a solid, ergonomic handle that doesn't slip. It hides as easily as a shadow but cuts hard and deep and fast.

I won't be throwing my blade like Violet.

Goddammit, I never should've let her stay at her own place.

I should've insisted. I should've reasoned better with her. Instead, I let her have her way, and now what?

I call security again but get nothing.

"Swear to God," I mutter under my breath. "If they don't have a good reason not to pick up this phone…"

I don't finish the sentence. Joe blanches and looks out the window as I drive so damn fast, rocks fly behind us, the ground whizzing past in a blur. I call Violet and Henri one at a time, over and over.

My phone buzzes with a text. I look quickly at the screen, but it isn't any of the people I want to hear from.

Armand: Boss, I think I found something of importance.

I don't respond. I don't have time for his bullshit right now. I would've fired him if I hadn't gotten distracted by Skylar's abduction.

"Tomorrow, you fire Armand's ass," I tell Joe.

He freezes but doesn't respond at first. I look over at him, and he seems to snap out of his stupor. "Armand?"

"Yes."

"Yes, sir. Will do."

I fill him in on everything, even why I'm here to check on her.

"Just so we're clear, sir. She was texting you, you asked if she was okay, and she didn't respond."

"Correct."

He seems to be mulling this over.

"Could she… have fallen asleep?"

I curse under my breath and push the gas pedal deeper. The roads whiz by us like they're on speed.

"If she did," I say with measured patience, "we'll leave well enough alone."

Again, he doesn't say anything but the silently raised eyebrows say it for him. He thinks I've lost my fucking mind.

He can think that, as long as he does what I tell him.

We're two minutes out when my phone buzzes again. I growl, glancing at the screen to see another text from Armand.

Armand: It's important, I think you should know

Jesus.

"Text Armand, tell him I'm driving, and ask him what the hell is going on that's so urgent."

Joe scowls and mutters a "yessir," already texting. No response at first. I pull up to Violet's house and park at the corner.

"You see anything?"

"No. You?"

I shake my head.

"But you don't know if it's one person or several we're looking for, what they look like..." his voice trails off.

"Correct."

A woman laughs on the other side of an open window, and a few teens sit on the stoop licking ice cream cones. A dog barks in the distance, and someone's lighting off fireworks a few blocks away. It looks just like any typical late summer night.

I walk up to her front door when the dumbass we saw earlier comes out. He's unsteady on his feet. Drunk.

"Ahh, Violet's lover," he says. Joe looks at me sharply.

"I'm her boss." She'd kill me for that, but she'd kill me faster for pretending to be her man. I'm not playing games right now.

"Right, like that matters," the asshole says with a snicker. "Why are you back?"

"I need to get into her apartment." There's no way on God's green earth he's going to make this easy on me. He'll need to be persuaded.

"And?"

"And I need you to let me upstairs."

He smirks at me and leans against the railing. "Can't do that without the pretty lady's say so. How do I know you didn't get into a fight and you're using me to get to her?"

Joe glances at me, ready to spring into action. I shake my head at him.

I want him all to myself.

Every second that passes places her in greater danger than before. The asshole that took those women moves fast, and I'm not fucking around.

In two seconds, I've got him by the collar, and I yank him inside the entryway where no one can see us. My MK3's pushed up to his neck, a bead of blood coloring the blade.

"Hey, man!" he says, panicking like a girl. "Hey!"

"Let me in and do it now. You do not call the cops unless you want a building inspector here by Monday. I've got connections in places you really, *really* don't want to go and will have this place condemned before you can wipe your ass."

I press the knife harder, drawing more blood.

"Jesus! Go!" he says in a strangled voice, stepping aside and handing me a set of keys. "Her key's the purple one, 208."

I toss him to Joe. "You escort him out of here and make sure he doesn't cause trouble."

Joe's grin is chilling, even to me. "My pleasure."

I take the stairs two at a time, listening. Something crashes inside her apartment. I double-time it.

She's got a deadbolt on the door, and I can't open it. It's reinforced steel, no goddamn way I can knock it down. I grab the key and shove it in the lock, then unfasten the deadbolt. The door falls open. I enter, Ruger in hand, and kick the door shut behind me.

My gaze slashes across her kitchen. Nothing.

Living room. Nothing.

Goddamn it, if I find her asleep in bed after all this—

I hear a scream and a growl, and I take off at a run down the hall. I try the door to her bedroom and find that locked, too. Too many keys on this goddamn key ring to find the right one, but this door's a basic wooden one.

I come at it full force, my shoulder slamming into it. Once. Twice. On the third hit, I knock it down, and it splinters like kindling. Violet turns to look at me, a pink handprint across her cheek and blood streaming down the side of her face. The hand holding her knife shakes. A curtain on her window flutters in the breeze.

"He got away!"

No.

I'll kill him.

Her voice quakes, her hand's trembling. I fight the need to hold her, to make sure she's okay, that she isn't hurt worse than it looks, but I can't let the fucker get away. I move past her and crane my neck out the window, just in time to see red brake lights on a small Mazda as it peels around the corner.

"*Motherfucker.* Did you see him?"

She nods, her eyes filling with tears, and she swipes them angrily away. "I did. It's the guy I found tonight in my search, the same goddamn guy they suspect for all those crimes but haven't been able to prove."

Okay, alright. She'll come back to my place, and we'll clean her up and find out what she knows. Who he is. We'll make sure she's okay.

"You're not safe here."

She winces. When she blinks, a tear rolls down her cheek, mingling with the blood. *Fuck.* "I had him. I fucking *had him*," she says.

"Are you hurt?"

"No," she says, vibrating with anger. "I'm *furious.*"

It's anger, then, that makes her cry.

She could be in shock. She could be injured. We've got more evidence now so we can track him down and find him, but first I have to make sure she's okay.

"Sit down."

She looks from me to the window, then back again. With effort, I gentle my voice. "Sit. Please."

It kills me to see those eyes of hers filled with tears. She cries, letting the tears go unchecked, and finally sits down. I don't realize until I kneel in front of her that I'm shaking.

"Oh God, you've got… you came in with a knife and a gun?"

I look down to see my Ruger in one hand and my MK3 in the other. I lay them down.

"Yeah, I have a tendency to overdo shit," I say, just to calm her down. If the motherfucker was in front of me now, I would wish I had more than this on me. "You alright? Do you need immediate medical attention?"

She stretches for a tissue from her bedside table but doesn't quite reach it. I hand her one silently.

"No, I'm okay." She continues to swipe angrily at the tears.

I want to kiss her, blood and sweat and tears and all. I want to haul her up into my arms and carry her away from this shitty apartment, bring her to my place, and treat her to the lap of luxury. I want her body to soften underneath me, to yield to everything and anything I want to do to her. But I can't do that to her. I can't do that *for* her. She's the type of woman who'd feel belittled if I treated her that way.

We'll get there.

I need to make her feel safe. I need her to trust me.

"Alright, woman." I reach for the box of tissues and place it beside her. "Tell me everything."

CHAPTER 10

Violet

I'M SO angry with myself I could cry. Hell, I realize when I swipe my hand across my eyes and find my fingers covered in blood and tears... I *am* crying.

Arrggh. *I do not cry.*

The only time I *do* cry is when my anger doesn't have an outlet. I ball up the tissues he hands me, desperate for some sort of release.

He's gone off to the bathroom to fetch a first aid kit and returns with a frown and the tiny plastic generic kit I got at a discount store. "You call this a first aid kit?"

I roll my eyes at him. "I don't usually get into a knife fight with intruders, Mr. Master. I get bruises from training and things like *paper cuts.* Like normal people."

His eyes gentle as he kneels in front of me again, and I'm momentarily struck by the enormity of this. He's so huge, even when he kneels, his head nearly comes to my shoulders. But something tells me he isn't a guy that kneels very often.

"Normal? Violet, you're anything but normal."

I like my name on his lips, like spiced honey. I snort out loud to cover the way my heart speeds up. "As *if*."

He quirks a brow at me and doesn't take the bait.

"So let's hear it."

"Okay, so I came home and I did inspect the place. Promise. Everywhere. And yes, Mr. Master, like a good girl I checked every room to make sure no one was here, and the coast was clear."

"Very good. And call me Cain."

I want to reach to his chin and run my finger along the stubble. Make him look at me. Instead, he's fumbling through the kit and pulling things out.

"Cain." I like the feel of his name in my mouth. "You're named after the world's first murderer."

A wry smile ghosts across his lips before he sobers again. "Something my mother never let me forget."

"It was intentional, then?"

"Yes." A flicker crosses his gaze before he shutters it again. "Now back to the story, Miss Price."

I want to hear him say my name, the word like a seductive caress.

"No more Miss Price either, please."

"Alright, Violet." Such a small thing, hearing my name from him, but the way he says it sounds like a poem. He lines up gauze, antibacterial wipes, and bandages. "Now. Everything."

I speak quickly. We need to move. I know more about who might have his sister, and I don't want to waste any more time.

"After I knew no one was here, I used the bathroom, when I heard a crash." Those eyes of his are fixed on me with an intensity that I feel straight to my belly. "I came in here to check, but there was no one here. The window was open, and a curtain was kinda blowing with the wind, but the room was empty."

"Did you open the window?"

"No. I looked out the window and saw no one. Nothing at all. I assumed I'd forgotten to close it and went out to the kitchen."

He makes a noise that sounds like a growl, but waits for me to continue. For a big, grumpy guy he can be patient when he wants to be.

I give him a curious look. "Wait, how did you know what I liked?"

"Stick with the story, please. You answer my questions first, then I'll answer yours." He tears open a gauze pad and gently swipes across my temple. He pulls it away stained in blood. I continue.

"I texted you, and then when I turned around there were irises on my windowsill."

"That weren't there before."

"No."

The savage cruelty I saw in his eyes when I first met him returns. I draw in a ragged breath. I look into his clear, sapphire eyes that glimmer like ice, the same frigid eyes that pulled the trigger next to a man's temple today without remorse. He watched that man crumple to the floor without blinking, then called for his team.

It was apparent to me from the moment I met him that fury and power war within him. He's only played nice for a little while.

Today I saw the real Cain Master.

With military precision, he slides a bandage open, then cradles the back of my head. The whole base of my skull fits easily in his cupped palm. With gentle pressure, he pulls me toward him as he puts the bandage on my cut. My breath catches at how gentle and careful he is, like he knows I'm injured and can't bear to cause me any more pain.

If only he knew.

I shiver.

His heavy brows draw over his eyes, and his mouth forms a thin, angry line.

"Go on."

He opens another antiseptic packet and lifts my hand in his. My hand looks so small engulfed in his much larger hands. Mine are bleeding. I don't remember why. The adrenaline and fear blinded me.

I draw in a shaky breath as he wipes the grit and blood from my hands. It stings, but I don't let myself flinch. "After I saw the flowers, I put my phone down. I considered calling you. I decided I was going to drive to your place after all, and when I came into my room, someone hit me."

He lets loose a string of curses.

I want to find the man who attacked me. I want to find him, and I want to kill him. I want him to pay for everything he's done. So I speed up my story.

"I felt the blow and blocked on instinct with a slip." It was drilled into me how to block a kick or punch, arms up to defend the face while squatting to block the gut.

He nods.

"When he was on the downswing, I turned and jabbed him straight in the gut."

"Did you get any names in your research?"

"Just Derrick Dossier, the man suspected but released on the rape and abduction charges."

Cain picks up his phone and makes a call. "I want you to get everything you can on Derrick Dossier.

Report on my desk within the hour." He doesn't even wait for a response but hangs up his phone and shoves it back in his pocket.

"This motherfucker's playing us. He's after you and may have my sister. We can't fuck around anymore, Violet."

There's my name again.

"Yeah. I'm coming back with you. We need to put our heads together. Pool resources."

He narrows his eyes. "What a novel concept. Pack a fucking bag."

"Do you ever say please?"

He looks down, his eyes on my shins. I'm wearing a pair of shorts, my legs on full display. Angry purple bruises mark my shins from earlier.

"Did you get these from my truck?"

"Yeah, your truck can be pretty damn aggressive."

He lifts one of my legs in his hands, cradling it just like he did my head. My heart beats faster at the rough feel of his hands on my skin and the way his brows draw together angrily, his mouth pressed tightly in a harsh frown. That focused, steady gaze unwavering.

He bends. My breath freezes. In shock, I don't breathe when he places a tender kiss on my legs, his lips brushing across the black and blue so tenderly it's barely more than a whisper. When I start breathing again, I'm acutely aware of the sound.

We don't speak. Seconds tick by, the only sounds in the room are my heavier breathing and his gentle, fluttering kisses across my skin.

If he looks at me, there's no turning back. If his eyes meet mine, I can't tell him no.

He lets me go. I shiver at the loss of his warmth.

He stands and walks away from me.

I'm saved.

Then why do I feel so disappointed?

"I'm sorry. We have to get out of here. On second thought, you're not packing. I'll buy you whatever you need. We're leaving now, and you'll tell me the rest of what happened on the way back."

"I can pack in less than a minute." I'm already on my way to the closet. I need to walk away from him.

He grumbles but uses the time to toss the bandage wrappers away. I grab a quilted backpack Candi gave me from the back of my closet and quickly shove folded clothes, underwear, a pair of sneakers, and my phone in the bag. He's waiting for me, his arms crossed over his chest. "Can you find the little pink bottle of lotion on the bedside table, please?"

I need to distract him so he doesn't see what I grab next. *No one* sees that, not even Candi.

"I can get you as many little pink bottles of lotion as your heart desires, let's go."

"That's a special one, it was for Candi's bachelorette party."

I got it as a freebie in the mail. I hope he doesn't see through the lie.

Another grumble, but he fetches it just in time. I yank the zipper on my bag closed and get to my feet.

"You had a guard here, didn't you?"

"Yes."

"I didn't need—"

"You fucking did, and he better have a good excuse as to why he didn't do his goddamn job." He slams the drawer closed and turns to stalk over to me.

I could never, *ever* be with a man like him. *Do this, do that.* He's about as supple as a steel rod, and I have to remember that.

They call him the executioner.

I can't let the gentle side of him mess with my mind. That's where women go wrong. They know in their heart a guy's no good for them. They *know* it. Yet something he does makes them forget all logic and they believe the stupid lie that they have a magical pussy that somehow cures all, that he won't ever drink/steal/lie again, or whatever the heck they tell themselves.

I won't let that happen.

When my mind wants to replay the feel of his full, hot lips on my aching skin, I shove it away. When my brain wants me to remember that he came to find me, that I didn't respond to his text and he knew I was in trouble and he *came for me,* I don't let myself dwell.

He's dangerous, ruthless, and arrogant, and so bad for me he's poison.

Poison.

When we exit the building, I try to hide my fear. Logically, I know there is no madman waiting for me outside, but it still feels like there could be.

I don't miss how he walks beside me. His razor-sharp gaze notes everything. If there's anyone here to try to take me now, they'd better have backup, a hand grenade, and a cannon, because no one's getting me without a declaration of war.

The ride back to his house hurts like *hell.*

"You've got ibuprofen back at that mansion, right?" I mutter, my head falling on the seat behind me. My eyes close.

"No sleeping," Cain snaps. My eyes fly back open.

"You really are a slave driver!"

That gets Joe's attention, but he doesn't say anything.

"You can't sleep now. You could have a concussion."

"Fine. But God, am I tired. How long do I have to stay awake?"

"Until the doctor gives you clearance."

"Oh God. I'm gonna need a coffee. Double shot of espresso, straight up."

"Need me to stop and get some?"

I sigh. "No. I don't drink coffee."

He shakes his head.

"What?"

He changes the subject. "Back to what happened."

"So I got him with a jab. I believe that's where we left off."

"You have a mean jab," Joe chimes in.

I stare at him. He's never seen me fight.

"How do you know?"

He shrugs and laughs. "I can just tell. You're a fighter. Little fireplug."

He's lying. I look at Cain, but his face is a mask of stone.

"I threw a jab and he fell back, and he would've gotten me but I aimed a very, *very* well-placed kick to his crotch that was *meant* to incapacitate him. And that was when everything began to go wrong."

Cain sighs and accelerates.

"This car is gorgeous, by the way. *Stunning*, with this all-leather interior. Are these heated seats?"

"Yes. Thank you. Get back to the story."

"There's not much more to tell. He rebounded, slapped me across the face so hard I bit my lip, and we literally brawled. I tried to pull my knife, but I was too slow, and by the time I got it out…" I sigh. I hate this part of the story. "He was out the window and onto the fire escape."

Cain frowns. "He slapped you?"

I nod. Of all those details I just told him, that's what he thinks about? "Yeah."

His back goes rigid.

"Remember I said you'll be at my place at eight a.m.? Now that order's null and void, since you're coming back with me."

Order? I think sometimes he forgets he's not my commander.

"Yesss…?"

Where's he going with this?

"Scratch that. Tomorrow morning at seven a.m., unless we have a breakthrough and find something we need to pursue, you'll get your first lesson in how to handle a gun."

I stifle a squeal. I've wanted to learn how to shoot a gun forever but haven't taken the time to do it.

"You have a trainer?"

He frowns, those glacial eyes glancing my way before he looks back to the road. "Yeah."

Joe chuckles softly. Is this an inside joke or something?

"Did you find anything before all this happened?" Cain asks, and his eyes meet mine in the rearview mirror. Something like camaraderie flashes between us, so quickly I wonder if it's my imagination.

He doesn't like that I was alone in the apartment and attacked. He wishes he was there.

Why does it excite me to imagine what would've happened if he was?

I should be appalled that he shot a man today. Without remorse. Without hesitation.

I'm not, though. In fact, quite the opposite.

It's the single most attractive thing he's done since I've met him. He's the man who could help me, and will.

What on earth does a guy like him find attractive about a girl like me? *What?*

Maybe I need to play into this. Maybe, if he were attracted to me...

No.

No, no, no. I've gotten this far without whoring myself out, and I won't start now.

Something tells me he'd make it worth my while...

"You mean, did I do any research? Damn right I did, and I have a list of leads we need to pursue as soon as possible. Has anyone contacted you about your sister?"

"No."

"Have you checked all your social media accounts and email and phone number?"

Again, the flash of stunning blue in the mirror. "Check my social media?"

"Do you… have social media?"

"No."

"Well, that makes things simpler."

I look out the window and Joe chuckles again, so softly I barely hear him, but the sound is unmistakable. What's so funny?

"When we get back, you'll see the doctor and we'll make sure you meet with my team. We'll combine what we've found so far." He glances in his rearview mirror again, but he doesn't look at me this time.

"Someone following us?"

A long gaze in the mirror again, and he finally shakes his head. "No."

The interior of the car is a soft, matte black leather, luxurious and decadent. The carpet's pristine, the windows and chrome details like new. More notable is the way it drives, though, so seamlessly you don't know it's accelerating until the world flies by you. So sleek, it cuts through the air with military precision.

"Is this your getaway car?"

"It is."

"The next time you rob a bank, I'll be your getaway driver."

"What's your going rate?"

"Oh, for you, I'd cut you a break and let it go for a cool mil."

He nods, as if thinking this over. "You're right. I *would* consider that a good deal."

"Take him for two," Joe chimes in over his shoulder. Cain almost smiles. His lips thin before the smile reaches his eyes.

Almost.

"So this is how you got to my place so quickly. You must've been driving like over a hundred miles an hour."

He doesn't reply, only gives me a slow, lazy shrug, like driving at the speed of light is seriously no big deal.

"So why so much slower now?"

He doesn't answer. Joe speaks up from the passenger seat. "We've got cargo now."

Cargo?

Oh.

Oh.

Me. I'm cargo.

Well then.

I think as a woman I should be offended by that, but somehow, I feel it's almost sweet.

And it's definitely something I could use to my advantage.

It's warm and comfortable here. I lean back against the seat, my senses overwhelmed with the rich scent of leather. I took ibuprofen from the first aid kit before we left to dull the pain, and it's kicked in, my bruises and scrapes no longer throbbing.

I've had bullshit luck with this kinda thing lately. Between the accident and this, I'm almost ready for a nice, boring day in the office—

Who'm I kidding? I'd stab myself in the eye with a pencil.

What I'm really ready for is some adventure that doesn't involve Violet Price, punching bag, as the main attraction.

I'm floating, and it's comfortable here, and for once in a very, very long time, I know that no one's going to hurt me.

"Do *not* fall asleep!"

I snap to attention, my eyes flying open. The next second, a surge of adrenaline powers through me and I glare at Cain in the rearview mirror.

"I'm not sleeping."

"You aren't *now*."

I can't believe I ever thought of seducing a guy like him. I would strangle him in his sleep.

We pull into the long driveway that leads to his garage. The house is alight. His team's awake.

I want to sleep. I was exhausted *before* all this, and now I'm at the point of no return. I'm so tired I could cry.

I open the door and shiver with a gust of night wind. I wrap my arms around myself and follow them both into the house.

It's different tonight than it was last night. Tonight, even though it's way past midnight, the place is teeming with people. Even Alma, his housekeeper, is in the kitchen in her robe, putting a kettle on the stove.

"Good evening," she says to me pleasantly. "Tea? Coffee?"

"Tea would be great, thank you."

In the kitchen, right up next to the counter, are large, padded, spindle chairs. They're so fun, they make me want to play music on a jukebox and wear a poodle skirt. But right now, every one of them is occupied by one of Cain's employees.

A bowl of popcorn, nothing left but kernels, sits on one side of the counter, and on the other, there's a large platter of cheese and a fruit tray pretty well picked over beside empty pizza boxes and energy drink empties. Laptops and notebooks are scattered about, and in one corner of the room, a series of monitors are set up.

Cain grabs a mug. Strange he doesn't let his house help get it.

Something's changed between us. Something... shifted... from the very first moment his lips touched my skin back in my apartment.

Hell, it was before that.

From the very first time I stared into his eyes after he'd ended a man's life.

"How do you take your tea?"

"Dash of milk, please."

He places it in front of me while the milk still swirls, and I sip. It's so hot it scalds the roof of the mouth, but somehow it's exactly what I need right now. I wrap my hands around the ceramic mug, the heat of it warming me through. One small comfort on a day fraught with violence.

Cain clears his throat. The room stills.

"For those who haven't met her yet, this is Violet Price, a new contractor who will be working for Master Enterprises in the short-term. Violet's skilled in kickboxing and knife throwing, speaks multiple languages, and will be a valuable asset to our team."

I look around the small group. The man who hit my car last night isn't here.

A few of them murmur greetings and some nod to me.

"Violet and I are in pursuit of someone we believe kidnapped my sister. We have reason to believe the man's a serial rapist who intends on abusing, possibly even fatally hurting, Skylar and that the same person has hinted at coming after her next. Tonight, she had an intruder in her apartment. She'll be here indefinitely, while we search for Skylar."

I take another sip of tea, not quite as hot now as it was before.

"Violet, are you in a position where you are ready to talk?" Cain gives me a curious look. I don't know what he means. Why wouldn't I be in a position to talk?

I look at him in surprise, as I finish my mug of tea and place it on the counter. His housekeeper scoops it up with a smile and stashes it in the dishwasher before I've put my hand back in my lap.

Okay, I could totally see why having a housekeeper is a good thing.

"What do you mean?"

He crosses the room to me, all fluid grace and muscle despite his bulk, and leans across the counter on his arm, speaking in a low rumble. "You okay? Or do you need some time to yourself?"

"I'm fine," I lie, my voice distant while my heart beats a thunderous beat in my chest. I can handle his arrogance and anger, but concern… now that's another story.

He nods. "Then why don't you fill us in."

CHAPTER 11

Violet

AN HOUR LATER, we wrap up for the night. Cain calls it "taking a break," giving me a good idea of what it's like to work with him. I'm not surprised, though. With his background, he's used to working in godawful conditions at any hour he needs.

I saw the doctor, a rather short, stocky woman with wiry black hair graying at the temples and thick, round glasses. She was brief. She pronounced me banged up but otherwise unharmed, her examination taking place around me talking over her shoulder at the guys.

"Someone already bandaged you up pretty well," she said. When I told her it was Cain, she didn't respond.

His team has a list of details to investigate, and we're trying to get a read on Dossier. I want to stay up and help, but my eyes feel so heavy I can hardly keep them open.

We have work to do. I have to let his team handle it.

I gave them my information. I don't want to put this down right now, but I can hardly keep my damn eyes open.

The bartender told us they were going to Canada. A lie, maybe?

Derrick Dossier has no listed address, no job that we can find, and virtually nothing to lead us to where we might find him. Honestly, the rest of the details begin to meld into my brain. I'm so tired, I feel like I'm starting to short-circuit.

Cain's standing by Joe, his arms crossed on his chest. I'm behind him on one of the stools, trying to sit upright before I keel right over. He looks over his shoulder at me, then turns around and faces me.

"You need to get to bed."

I yawn widely and want to protest like a small, petulant child. *I'm not tired.* But I'm no good to anyone if I can't see straight.

"Yeah."

I go to pick up my bag, but he reaches for it and swings it over his shoulder. I'm in no mood to fight with him, so I let him. Without a word, he slides his hand over the small of my back.

A moment ago I felt like I could fall asleep and not wake up until Christmas. Now, I'm suddenly very, very awake.

We were pretending earlier that I meant something to him. Why's he doing this now? A part of me wants to pull away, and another part of me realizes that stumbling right now would only make me look foolish.

"This way," he says, like the only reason he's got his hand on my back is so he can show me where to go.

Very interesting, Mr. Master. Very interesting indeed.

He leads me to a staircase I've only seen from a distance. I stare at the steep, hardwood stairs and briefly consider asking if he'll let me sling myself up on his back, but that seems kinda desperate, and I don't even have the energy to do that.

When he takes his hand off my back, I wobble a little. I'm vaguely aware of him frowning at me;, I push myself to move, to put one foot in front of the other, but every step feels like my feet are getting heavier.

Finally, we reach the top of the stairs. My vision blurs as he steps to the left. "This way."

In my mind's eye, his voice is the low rumble of volcanoes churning. I follow the rumble automatically.

"Why so far?" I ask, my words slurred. I'd sleep on the damn landing at this point. That carpet looks pretty inviting.

"Just about there," he says almost gently, in that tone he used earlier. "I want your room near mine."

Of course he does.

He stops short, and like an idiot, I don't stop in time. I crash into his back like I've just learned how to walk. He turns and catches me as I wobble on my feet.

"Sorry."

"Christ, woman," he says in a low rumble. Without a word, he does what I wanted him to do but had been too proud to ask. He bends, then effortlessly lifts me, my feet dangling and my head lolling to the side on his chest.

"Well, this is a nice office perk." I sound like I'm drunk.

That earns me another grumble.

The door to the room is open, but I hardly notice. My senses are on overload, and every damn detail is filled with *him*. The masculine scent of him, raw and primal. The broad stretch of his muscled shoulders exposed because he's wearing a tank, his stubble thicker now that it's so late in the day. The heavy sound of his breathing.

Can he hear how fast my heart beats? Can he feel the way my skin heats?

Can he see the flush that creeps over my body because we're touching?

I'm intoxicated from lack of sleep and adrenaline from all the events of the day.

I try to keep my body erect so my head doesn't snuggle up in that hollow of his neck like I want it to. "You're crossing a line here, you know."

"Doing what?"

Thump goes my heart. "Touching me."

A beat passes before he responds. "I know." It's dark in here save for the yellowed pool of a nightlight beside the bed, but even with the shades drawn and lights dimmed, I can tell this room's outfitted in luxury. I don't care.

He could have had one of his men show me the way. He could have pointed or gestured or even just walked beside me.

I need him. I need what his team can do for me. I have to make sure I don't say or do anything that jeopardizes what I need.

He's still holding me. I'm barely breathing, afraid if I move too quickly, I'll wake and find I was only dreaming.

Men don't touch women like me, and those that even think about it face the consequences.

I want him to know it's okay, or maybe I just want to assure myself.

So I reach my hand to his jaw and do what I wanted to from the first time I saw him. I lay my hand on his stubbled jaw, thrilled at the prickly feel.

"I'll help you find your sister," I whisper.

Heat flares in his eyes. "You will. And we'll find your parents' killers."

I swallow, not sure what else to say.

I have to get ahold of myself.

"You could put me down, now." My voice doesn't sound like my own, all breathy and whispery yet somehow husky. I feel… *sexy.*

How does he make me feel sexy?

"I could."

Still, he doesn't.

I want him to kiss me, but there's no telling what will happen if he does.

Just a kiss, I taunt myself. *What harm could come from a kiss?*

His eyes spark at me, like he's reading my mind. Maybe he can, I think in my sleepy state. He's already larger than life and fearless. It only makes sense that he has superhuman abilities too.

I feel as if I'm standing on the edge of a precipice. One gust of wind, and I'll plummet to my death.

But I've always been more afraid of complacency than taking chances.

Slowly, so slowly at first I think it's my woozy, exhausted imagination, he bends his head a bit closer to me. I stare at his full, gorgeous lips, and imagine what it would be like to lick and bite them. I wonder what he tastes like.

Fire licks through me.

My eyes rove over his stubble, then down to his neck. I watch him swallow. The cuts he sustained are no longer bleeding, but the skin's an angry red between his collarbone and neck.

"You're hurt," I say in a hushed tone. And before I know what I'm doing, my hands are at his neck to anchor myself and I'm pulling myself closer to him. My lips meet his skin, kissing it better. I feel like I could cry.

The energy between the two of us crackles and sizzles. I tremble at his nearness, at his scent. I want to *taste* him.

I close my eyes and go for broke. I lick where I just kissed.

The groan he utters lashes through me as his grip tightens. I suckle his skin. I want more. *I need* more. I swear I feel the *snap* as his resolve breaks.

His mouth is so close I can feel his breath. I'm on the bed. I don't even know how I got here. He kneels beside me, the bed sagging under his weight.

Strong fingers grasping my chin, he lifts my mouth from his neck, and for one heart-stopping moment, I don't know what terrifies me more—the thought of him kissing me or the thought of him turning away.

His fingers tangle in my hair as if to prove to himself that I'm real, that I can't get away from him. I watch his lips part. My heart slams against my rib cage... then his mouth meets mine and my thoughts come to a stuttering, screeching halt as my brain short-circuits and I fall fully into my body.

Like everything about Cain Master, his kiss is *too much.*

Too much everything.

My heart beats too fast, my breathing's too ragged, my body's on *fire* just from this one kiss. He tugs the lock of my hair wrapped around his fingers, pulling my head back, and when I gasp from the intensity of it, he takes advantage, moving to fully claim my mouth until there's no room for escape.

I want everything. *All* of him. His hands on my breasts, his naked body pressed to mine, his length inside me. *I want him in me.*

I want to live in this moment, revel in it. Every fiber of me's alive with excitement, need and desire rolling through me to the tips of my toes. I don't know if I'm awake or dreaming, but if it's a dream, I don't want to wake. If I'm awake, I don't want to fall asleep.

I squeeze my legs together as pressure builds between my thighs, a throbbing, burning need.

Something behind him blares like a foghorn. At first, he ignores it, but at the second raucous shriek, he pulls away. I stifle a whimper.

His goddamn phone.

"I have to take this." He slams his phone on and smacks it to his ear. All I have to say is, whoever's on the other end of that line better have something important to say or the both of us won't think twice about murder.

"What?"

I sit up, awake, but can't hear a thing.

He curses. "I'll be right there."

When he hangs up his phone and glares, I know his anger isn't meant for me. He doesn't like to be interrupted on a *good* day, never mind now.

"I have to go. We got a lead on another case we're working on." He runs a hand through his hair. I've never been so jealous of another person's fingers. "I need you to get some sleep. Tomorrow, we will investigate further, and you get your shooting lesson."

He turns to leave. I feel cold and hot all at once as I watch him. Before he goes, he looks over his shoulder at me.

"I'm sorry." I don't know if he's apologizing for leaving or for kissing me. Maybe both. "Shooting range is opposite the pool. Meet me there at seven."

The door shuts with finality.

I stare at it for a moment, wondering if everything that just happened was my imagination. My fingers roam to my lips, and my eyes flutter closed.

I did not imagine that.

He kissed me. He kissed me, and I want more.

Did I just sell my soul to the Devil?

CHAPTER 12

Cain

It's two o'clock in the morning when I finally get to bed. I signed off on a job involving several of my men, because I want them back here as soon as possible. Every other job we're working on needs to be finished, and quickly, and thank fuck we're closing in on one deal so I can free up more of my men. Tomorrow—Jesus, *today*—we need to make headway on finding Skylar.

But my mind's on the woman across the hall from me. It's a damn good thing I got the call when I did, or who knows where we would've ended up.

I don't regret it, though. I want her to know that I want her.

I whip off my clothes and climb into bed, ignoring the raging hard-on I still have from kissing her earlier. I need sleep before tomorrow. I punch my pillow, frustrated that she isn't beside me.

I close my eyes shut tight, willing myself to sleep. My body's fatigued, but it's something I'm so used to, I've trained myself to stay awake. Once, when I was stationed outside of Paris before the fiasco with the gendarmerie, I stayed awake for thirty-six hours straight, waiting for news from the White House. When I finally heard what I needed to and dozed off, we were under attack an hour later.

I'm no stranger to lack of sleep. Still, I need some or I'll be useless tomorrow.

I go over the day in my mind. Her coming to me, asking for the job.

I asked Armand to make her think it was her idea to come here. And he did. How was I to know he planned on fucking *risking her life* to do it?

I interrogated the shit out of him but didn't let him go until today. I'll have to follow up with Joe. My mind's focused on all things Violet.

Violet.

I need her out of my mind. I have to find Skylar, but we have no fucking leads.

Tomorrow, I'll burn the city of Salem to the ground to find her.

I close my eyes and see vivid violet eyes.

I remember the way her mouth tasted like berries and cream, fresh, sweet, and decadent. I remember the way her skin felt in my hands, warm, silk-wrapped seduction that I wanted to worship. I remember the way she yielded when I touched her, the only softness she may ever succumb to.

I never have trouble falling asleep. I train hard, I work hard, and when my head hits the pillow, I'm asleep. But tonight, I'm distracted by the woman lying in a bed only paces from my room, and guilty that I'm even thinking of her when my sister's in danger.

Why Skylar?

Why Violet?

I can't shake the feeling that it's someone after me, someone seeking to get revenge. The list of my enemies is as long as my arm, and I can't even begin to decipher who it could be. I never heard the name Derrick Dossier before tonight.

She promised she'd help me. I know she will. Together, we'll find Skylar.

I fall into a deep and dreamless sleep and don't move or wake until my alarm clock sounds a few hours later.

I stifle a groan and smack the alarm off, get to my feet, and head to the bathroom. Use the facilities, wash my face, scrub a hand through my hair. I sleep bare-chested, the dog tags I wear glinting in the bright overhead lighting. They aren't mine, but I won't take them off. They remind me of the man who made me who I am today, for better or for worse. They remind me how I got here.

Where's Skylar?

Is she hurt?

Is Violet?

Did she sleep well?

I don't drink, but for once, I understand the appeal of a Bloody-fucking-Mary.

I tug on a tee, jeans, and a pair of socks and boots, then check my phone.

No messages, which shouldn't be surprising since I only slept a few hours. I glance at the clock. Six thirty. She's supposed to meet me at the target range at seven.

I've got just enough time for a cup of coffee. The door to her room is shut tight, no sound from the other side. She might be tired, but so am I, and if she's working with me, she'll learn to deal with sleep deprivation. She'd better not be late.

The house is either wide awake or most of my staff never went to bed last night. I pay them well to work hard for long hours and give them all six weeks of paid leave throughout the year. I guarantee them the best benefits of any other private firm on the East Coast. They're loyal to the core.

A door slams in the distance, and I pause on the landing. Someone shouts, then Joe's voice—deeper, calmer—replies.

Armand? Did Joe do what I told him to?

I find Alma at the landing. She's already dressed for the day, her hair tucked into a solid blue bandana, a dustpan in hand. I tried to hire her just to do the cooking, but she insists on doing the cleaning as well. So, I hired a small staff to assist. This house is huge.

"Good morning, Mr. Master."

"Morning, Alma. What's all the noise?"

"I don't know, sir. I keep my business to myself, you know." She gives me a tight smile, swiping her rag along the side tables until they shine. She doesn't suffer dust or fingerprints. Someone could rob our place, and she'd have the prints wiped off before the cops could arrive.

Not that we'd need them.

"But I *think*," she says, turning so I can't see her face. I'm sure she's smiling, though, because she's always smiling. "Your little lady has already awoken."

My little lady?

She is little, I'll give her that.

"Has she?"

"Yessir. She came down earlier looking for a few things."

I'm walking down the stairs as Alma fills me in but have half an ear out for Armand and Joe.

"What was she looking for?"

"Cucumbers, filtered water, fresh mint, and some moisturizer." I'll have her make a list tonight of everything she needs.

"And?"

"I got her everything she requested, sir."

"Thank you."

The smell of coffee wafts past me, along with the low murmur of voices in the kitchen. I trot down the remaining steps and head to the kitchen. Violet's nowhere to be seen. Joe's sitting at the head of the table with a cup the size of a Great Lake in front of him, along with a few others. They all look up when I enter.

"Morning. Anyone seen Miss Price?"

"Morning, sir," Joe says, his eyes twinkling at me. "I believe Miss Price is ready for her... instruction?" He leaves enough of a pause between his words to make the other men guffaw. I'll give him a fucking lesson.

"At the shooting range?" I don't want her there without me. We've got weapons that would blow the arm off a giant.

"Yessir."

"She has no shooting experience. I don't want her at the range without someone who knows how to shoot."

"No shooting experience?" Joe looks baffled. He's probably wondering why I hired someone with no shooting experience, but I don't owe him an explanation.

On paper, she's got skills. She's got many things she can offer my team. In real life, I want a hell of a lot more than her skill set.

"I'm sorry, I didn't know. It won't happen again."

I nod. "Did you do what I asked you to?"

"Yessir." He was supposed to fire Armand this morning.

"I'm guessing that didn't go over so well?"

"No, not at all, but it confirmed for me you made the right call."

The other men watch us. Alma comes into the kitchen and grabs a broom, quickly sweeping up imaginary crumbs. "Did it?"

"Yessir."

I pour myself a steaming mug of coffee.

"And what was that?"

"That it was time for him to go." He frowns. "He had nothing but shit to say about all of us in his exit interview."

"Exit interview?"

"Yeah, my euphemism for the profanities he yelled on his way out the door."

Why am I not surprised? The clock on the kitchen wall chimes six forty-five. I need to meet her at the range.

"I'll arrange for his things to be boxed up and shipped. Your job's done. Thanks, Joe."

"Of course, sir."

"Do we have any more information on Skylar?" I'm standing by the door. I don't like that Armand left angry with us. He could compromise our operation with the right motives.

Joe shakes his head sadly. "No. I checked in with Lottie, and she still hasn't come home, but there's no evidence that whoever took her reached out to anyone."

My hand is on the door to go out.

"How about Derrick Dossier, anyone find any more information on him?"

"I found something encrypted on a server, and we're working on it. One thing to note is that it does appear he's former military, dishonorably discharged."

Dishonorably discharged. Just like me.

Christ.

We have a history together; I just don't know what the fuck it is yet. There's more to his name than appears.

"Call me the second you find anything."

"We have a list of the survivors, Mr. Master, and their addresses."

I turn around to look at Joe. The room's grown quiet, all eyes on me. "I want a printout when we get back from the shooting range."

Joe nods. "Yessir."

Today, we hunt for sources that lead us to Skylar.

Alma pulls a huge pan of steaming hot muffins out of the oven, and several of the men grab them before she can put them on a serving platter.

"*Dios mio!* You'll burn your fingers off. Leave some for your boss!"

I've told her a hundred times I don't eat breakfast, and still, she keeps trying.

Violet and I have an hour to practice before we go over the names and locations of the survivors. If we can interview them… we might find what we need after all.

I start to turn the doorknob but pause as Joe's phone rings, and he answers it. He frowns, his eyes coming straight at me. "You gave her a gun? And now the door to the target range is locked?

Jesus.

The kitchen door slams behind me with a bang.

CHAPTER 13

Violet

Oh God, he's going to absolutely fucking *murder* me for this, but it will be worth it. You only live once, so you might as well make that one time so worth it.

I tried to sleep last night and did end up finally catching some zzz's, but it was nowhere near enough. My mind was teeming with everything that had happened… and that kiss. So when I woke, I knew where I had to go.

I knew he was meeting me here. I asked in the kitchen about who the shooting instructor was, and by the way they all looked at each other knowingly and laughed, I knew it was Cain.

I wanted to get here ahead of him. I didn't want to give him even that little bit of control over me.

So I came here first, even though I don't know what I'm doing.

I guessed he doesn't just leave guns sitting around, but I found Joe in the kitchen, and I may have told a bit of a white lie embellished with what I knew Joe heard last night about our practice. Joe allowed me to come down here, but there was another guy, some big dude with a shaved head, training outside. He was the one that let me in.

The floor beneath my feet's sparkling clean, made of concrete. Each practice area, sectioned off like cubicles, has a place to stand, a small table covered in velvet where I'm presuming you lay your guns, a hook with headphone things, and in front, targets at a distance. Half a dozen people could safely practice in here at once.

He's coming here, coming soon, and my body heats with this knowledge. I want him so badly I can taste it. *I want so much more than a kiss.*

Even his attention's nice, and I know I'm going to get more than I can handle if he catches me in here. I'm early though, at least fifteen minutes. I'll put this all away before he comes.

I may have never shot a gun, but I'm no fool. I got a few hours of sleep, then pulled up a YouTube video on my phone and watched a series of "intro to shooting" videos. I didn't want to be a complete newb.

I just want to touch the guns. I just want to feel them in my hand, see how heavy they are.

I have to admit, I didn't know guns were so *gorgeous*.

I lift each gun, feeling the substantial weight of them in my palm. I don't know why I ever bothered with throwing knives when guns were an option. I caress the heavy barrels, finger the finely crafted details. I can't believe I've gone this long in my life without ever holding a gun. I've been missing out.

I doubt these are all the weapons he has on his property, but I'm pretty happy with what I can play around with for now.

There's a compact pistol that feels like I'm holding a stick of dynamite in my hands. I place it back in the box, gingerly. Whoa. That thing's deadly.

Next up, a revolver. Don't know the name but it's exquisite. I feel energy pulse through me, and for one brief moment, imagine electricity lighting up my veins like live wires. I'm not tired anymore when I hold the revolver.

There are handguns and shotguns, some that make me think of private investigators wearing suits and trench coats, others that look like they should be strapped to the backs of a military brigade.

I'm not dumb enough to load any of them. I put down the revolver and pick up another gun, imagine pointing it at the target. How hard is it to pull the trigger?

"Come at me," I whisper, remembering what Cain muttered at Troy last night, his words laden with a deadly threat. *"Come at me, bro."*

I pull the trigger just to see what it feels like.

Fire erupts from the gun.

I fall to the floor, too stunned at first to feel the pain in my shoulder. My ears ring from the deafening roar of the shot, and the instinctive fight or flight part of me feels like I should run for cover.

The door to the firing range bursts open, and I know before I even look to see who it is, Cain Master's entered the arena.

Great.

I am in so much damn trouble it isn't even funny.

I place the gun gingerly down on the ground—too little, too late?—and leap to my feet. "I had no idea it was loaded!" I say in my defense. I flail my arms defensively, so he doesn't actually murder me with his bare hands, but I suspect if he really wants to, my waving arms aren't going to hold him back.

I knew the first time I saw Cain that he was capable of anger. I knew it from the moment our eyes first met, when I saw a world of hurt and rage simmering in his eyes. I knew it when we began hunting for his sister, and I saw him control and harness that anger when he killed the bartender last night.

But this… this isn't controlled anger. It's nothing but unadulterated, boiling hot rage, and he's coming straight at me.

He has to stop at some point, I reason. He has to... stop walking and... *halt.*

But he doesn't.

When he reaches me, he grabs me by the upper arms and shakes me, hard enough to make my teeth rattle, before he shoves me up against the wall with a growl I feel deep in my belly. Cold concrete hits my back as his fingers grasp my chin. I've never wanted to look away from someone so badly in my life, but his grip on my chin makes that impossible.

He says something to me, but my ears are ringing from the sound of the shot and the blood pounding in my head. I shake my head to signal to him that I can't hear him.

He raises his voice so loudly, my stomach clenches.

"You think you can shoot a gun? With no training, no experience, nothing to keep you safe? Do you?" he snarls. A vein throbs in his temple, his nostrils flare. I cringe. What else am I supposed to do? I'm wilting under the heat of his glare, and I totally deserve this. Shooting a loaded gun is *really* fucking stupid. I wouldn't blame him if he made me leave or fired me or made me go peel potatoes in the kitchen, or whatever it is a military guy does to someone who's royally fucked up.

My voice shakes. "I didn't mean to. I didn't know it was loaded."

My ears still ring. I want to cover them to still the aching reverberation.

His eyes are sharp as ice, blue rivulets of churning fury, as he holds my gaze.

"Who gave you the gun?"

"I—I don't know his name. A guy with a shaved head? He was outside."

"Claude."

Still holding my gaze, he reaches for his cell phone and makes a call. I'm trembling, scared of what he'll do next, scared to say a thing. He puts it on speakerphone.

"Yes, sir?"

His voice cuts like a scalpel. "Did I give you permission to give Miss Price a weapon?"

A pause, then, "No sir."

"She did not have permission to touch a weapon, and I'll punish her for that. But if you ever again give anyone a weapon without my express consent, I will fire you. Consider this your one and only warning. Do you understand me?"

Punish?

"Yes, sir. Of course, sir. I'm so sorry."

"Miss Price, I believe you have something to say as well."

I'm shaking in his grip, and my voice sounds distant and muffled. "I'm sorry I asked you for a weapon. I'm sorry I got you in trouble."

I'm sorry I got myself in trouble?

Why did I think it was okay to work with him again?

I'm shaking as he hangs up the phone and shoves it back into his pocket, which, unfortunately, brings his furious gaze back to focus fully on *me*.

Gah-reat.

I open my mouth to speak, but I don't know what I'm going to say. I have to say… something. But when I go to speak, he shakes his head at me.

"No."

I don't know exactly what he's saying "no" to, but I clamp my mouth shut. It's convenient, since I don't know what I would say anyway.

I look down at his hands on my wrists and realize he's shackled me in his grip. With the cold concrete wall at my back, there isn't a single move I know that could get me out of this position. He dwarfs me, my whole body shadowed by his.

When he speaks, his voice vibrates with anger.

"Are you familiar with the Four-Step Approach to Progressive Discipline, Miss Price?"

Ouch. We've gone from the hottest kiss of my life to "Miss Price."

I shake my head, still not sure if I'm allowed to speak.

"Step one." His words travel down my neck to my collarbone and warm my skin. I swallow hard.

"Verbal warning. The supervisor tells the employee of their concerns and listens to the employee's side of the story, then issues a verbal warning of disciplinary actions." His fingers flex on my wrists.

I nod dumbly. Yes. Mhm. Got it.

"Step two," he growls. Oooh, boy. "Written warning. Self-explanatory, yes?"

"Yes, sir," I whisper. I don't have a submissive bone in my body but showing some respect right now might help my plight.

His eyes soften for a fraction of a second at my response. I feel about two feet tall and would feel about ten years old if my body didn't react the way it did to his intimidation tactics. My pulse races, and my mouth goes dry, remembering the last time we were this close to one another, what he'd done next.

I can't look away from his eyes and wish I could.

"Step three involves suspension. Paid or unpaid leave for a defined length of time, presumably during which the employee considers their behavior and decides how they will proceed."

A pause where neither of us speaks, before he finishes, "Step four is termination."

Silence can be loud sometimes. Right now, it's deafening.

He releases my wrists, but I still can't move, because he leans in on one forearm, his other caging me in. I'm just as secured as I was before.

This *may* not be the time to once again remind him that I'm not his employee, but an independent contractor.

"Do you know how many men I've let go, Miss Price?"

I shake my head.

"One. This morning. And do you know why?"

I shake my head again. I feel as if I'm going to cry.

"Because he could've killed you with his stupidity."

I can't breathe. I try but my lungs don't seem to want to work.

The man I affectionately called Douche… Armand, I think his name is… Fired. Because… he could've killed me?

I don't know why I mean anything at all to Cain. But there's no point in denying the fact that I do. Probably more than I deserve.

"I'm sorry," I repeat. "I really didn't know it was loaded."

His shoulders rise as he draws in a deep breath before he releases it. "The guns down here usually aren't loaded, because I want my men to bring their own ammo with them. We do have loaded guns on the premises, because the only people who ever set foot here are trained in weaponry and shooting, and because having loaded weapons on hand helps in matters of self-defense."

I nod. I don't know how else to respond.

"Lesson one. Always, *always* assume that a weapon in your hand is loaded."

I want to smack my own forehead with a resounding *duh*, because that sounds like something that should be obvious.

"How are your ears?"

"They're… okay."

"Lesson two." He's still holding his body pressed to mine, still pinning me to the wall. His breath skates across my skin, a reminder of what happened last night. My lips tingle. "You can permanently damage your hearing from *one* gunshot if you don't have proper protection. Always wear electronic earmuffs or ear plugs."

I nod.

His gaze travels down to my shoulder. "Did you hurt yourself on the kickback?"

I forgot about the pain until he mentioned it just now. *Ouch.* Tears sting my eyes, and not just from physical pain.

"Yes."

With a scowl that would freeze hell, he reaches for my collar and gently tries to tug down my T-shirt so he can inspect my shoulder. The collar's unyielding, though, and he can't see anything.

Frowning, he steps back and folds his arms across his chest like he's surveying me. "Off with the shirt."

I try to play this off. Lighten the mood, you could say, to take his focus away from my trembling hands and the way I'm flushing like I'm sunburnt.

"My, my, Mr. Master, so early in the morning and you're—"

"Not. Playing."

The flirtation dies on my lips as I reach for the bottom of my shirt. I try to tug it up so he can only see my shoulder, a really futile attempt at holding onto some semblance of control through this, but it's no use. With a sigh, I take it off. My shoulder *burns*.

"Of all the guns you could've shot, you chose the one with the quietest sound but meanest kickback."

"Right. Good one, Vi." I swallow my need to cry and wince when his fingers graze my shoulder.

I remember the way he kissed my bruised shins when he bandaged me yesterday. I remember the way he cradled my head and comforted me. While still obviously angry, he's no less gentle this time than he was the day before.

Sliding one hand along the small of my back, he braces me as he inspects my shoulder. "You shouldn't be bruised," he whispers. "These all happened on my watch. Never again."

Not all, I want to remind him. The car accident wasn't his fault. Hell, none of it is. Why does he blame himself?

"You don't need to see a doctor for this, but we should wait on any more practice for today."

I shake my head. "No. No, please, Cain. I'm fine." I move my arm around just to show him I'm okay, but I can't hide the wince when pain explodes along my arm and shoulder.

"The hell you are."

I watch his gaze rove hungrily over my barely clad breasts and flat belly before I yank my shirt back on.

"I need to learn how to shoot! I need you to teach me."

"You do not make demands around here, Miss Price."

Fuck him with the Miss Price bullshit.

"I'm not Miss Price!" I yell in a fit of frustration. "My name is *Violet*!"

Something snaps in him. I see it in his eyes. One minute, he's staring at me angrily, prepared to argue with me. The next, there's cold decision in his gaze.

"You want me to teach you?" he asks, his voice an alarming purr. "Fine. I'll teach you."

His words ring in my memory.

I'll punish her for that.

"The gun on your left is the perfect gun for beginner's practice. Lift it with two hands and point it *away* from you and repeat the first rule I told you."

I nod. "Always assume a gun is loaded."

"*Always.* Do what I said and place it on the table in front of you." Ahead of us are the targets, a few bullseyes, but most covered in thick paper in the shape of a human body.

My hand shakes a little, but I will the trembling to stop. I pick up the gun, point it away from me, and lay it on the velvet table in my cubicle. My hands hang by my sides awkwardly.

"Good. Now lean over the table on your forearms."

I blink. "Lean over the table?" What the hell does that have to do with holding a gun?

His icy blue stare pins me in place. "Lean. Over. The. Table."

I turn away from him, shaking, as I do what he tells me. I hear him walk up to me right before I feel his heat at my back. I still when he leans over me, pushing me against the table while he reaches for something I didn't see before–small leather loops on the table, no doubt meant to secure weapons when they're not in use. Only it isn't the gun he's securing.

"Cain! What are you doing?" I hate that my voice shakes. Hate that he's scaring me.

Without a word, he slips my wrist in the first leather harness, then the next.

Click. I can't move my arms. I'm bent over the velvet table, my wrists secured in front of me.

"The target range is soundproof, Violet. No one will hear you if you scream. So go ahead. Scream to your little heart's content. I'll enjoy this more if you do."

If he didn't have his hand on my lower back just now, I'd be terrified. As it is, I wouldn't say I'm exactly at ease…

I hear the click of metal, a swish. Is he… unfastening his jeans? What?

My hands shake, and my belly quivers. I…what will he…

"Repeat rule number one, Violet."

I love the way he says my name.

I swallow, my voice still distant even as the ringing fades. "Always assume a gun is loaded."

"Maybe this will help burn it into your memory." There's the sound of a swish, then a line of fire lights up my ass. I gasp, too shocked to do more than that. I whip my head around to see him standing behind me, his belt folded over in his grip.

Heat fans my core while indignation rises.

I could tell him off. I could tell him to go fuck himself and keep his big hands to himself. But then I'm fucked. Then I'm back to square one, where I've been for so long the very thought of going back there makes me feel desperate. No. No, I can't walk away from him, not now. Not when I've come so close to what I need.

I catch his gaze for one heart-stopping moment. I'm the utter focus of his attention. A bomb could go off beside him right now and his attention wouldn't waver.

His icy voice shatters the silence. "Did I give you permission to turn around?"

I hold his gaze. Is he... into this?

Am I?

I shake my head wordlessly. He makes a twirly motion with his finger and points. "Then turn back around and stay bent over that table." I didn't even realize I'd stood up, hunched over as my wrists are still secured.

Shaking, I do what he says.

"Tell me rule number two."

I cringe, knowing he's going to punish me now, somehow craving and dreading it at the same time. "Always wear ear protection."

Again, the whir of leather and another searing strike. I cry out this time, but before I can recover there's an additional lash of leather.

Rule number two. Two strikes.

I bite my lip. Even though it hurts, I know a man as strong as he is could tear the skin off my back if he whipped me at full strength. He's moderating his strength, by a lot.

"Earmuffs on." He's right up next to me when he slides them over my ears. The ringing stops, but all other sounds are muffled.

His voice sounds as if it's far, far off in the distance.

He's still standing behind me. I can feel his eyes burning through me as vividly as his belt.

"Rule number three."

Oh, God, will that be three strikes?

"*Always* keep your finger on the outside of the trigger guard, nowhere near the trigger, until you're ready to shoot."

Leaning across my body, he slides the gun between my secured wrists. "Show me."

I make sure my fingers are nowhere near the trigger.

He nods. "Good. Just like that." He takes the gun away. "Bend over the table."

"Oh my God! Again?"

"You didn't really think we were done, did you?"

I ignore the way excitement builds in my belly, because I don't have any fucking idea why the knowledge that he's going to continue to punish me thrills me.

I shake my head numbly. I bend over the table again. This time, I squeeze my eyes shut tight.

No warning at all, but his belt lands with rapid precision, each line of fire building on the one before it until my body screams in pain.

One.

Two.

Three.

Then he's in my space, his body over mine and his pelvis pressed up against my aching, heated ass. I look down at his large hands placed on either side of me and shiver. I feel his prickly stubble along my cheek as his mouth comes to my ear. "Did you learn your lesson, Violet?" His teeth clench on my earlobe, and I hiss in a breath.

Heat races through me. I close my eyes. I'm drowning in him, in his nearness and dominance, his voice and clean, masculine scent. My heart beats along with his as he's pressed up against my back.

"Yes, sir."

"Tell me something, then."

"Yes?" I whisper.

"If I slid my fingers into your panties, would I find you wet?"

My mouth falls open. "What?"

"I spanked you."

That felt like more than a spanking. My voice trembles. "You call that a spanking? A spanking is over your lap with your palm."

"I can arrange that, too."

Gah! I think I swallowed my tongue.

"Cain!"

"*Violet*. Did your punishment turn you on?"

In my trademark nonsensical way, I answer a question with a question. "If that was punishment, would I be in trouble for being turned on?"

"Of course. You'd have to wait until I got you alone later to do anything about that." I slam my lips together so I don't do something stupid like beg.

I feel his hands anchored on my hips and he draws me closer to him. His erection presses up against my ass.

I'm not the only one turned on.

He unfastens the cuffs, turns me around to face him, then slides his hand along my jaw, his anger dialed back to a low simmer.

"Today's lesson's over, but we're nowhere near done here. We have unfinished business, you and I. Understood?"

I nod. "Yes."

"Tomorrow morning, you'll meet me here at seven a.m. You do not enter until I am here. You do not pick up a weapon until you have permission. You do not shoot a gun without my permission. And I'll be sure to help you remember each rule."

I nod again. Does that mean he'll… turn this into what I think he will?

How will I focus when he's doing *that?*

I wish our lesson wasn't over for the day, but I'm not sure how much more I can take. I'm already turned on beyond reason, so much I'm shaking.

People always say I'm intense. Some can't handle my brand of intensity. They want me to play nice, to follow the rules. They like things like polite conversation and social norms. Not me, though. That's never been who I am.

I once dated a guy who got angry with me when I wouldn't let him pull out my chair or order dinner for me. I told him I take care of myself, and I'm not giving that up for a guy I hardly know. "You're too intense," he said when he dropped me back off at my apartment.

Too intense.

I held those words within me. I remembered them. And when I found myself alone, or wishing for some kind of companionship, I'd pull them up again.

Too intense.

I was too intense for anyone to ever love.

"Where'd you go just now?" Cain asks, his sapphire eyes boring into mine. "You sometimes go somewhere in your mind, like you're dredging up memories. Where'd you go this time?"

There's no need to hide the truth.

"I was just thinking that... until I met you, I'd never met anyone more intense than I am."

A glimmer of a smile that doesn't reach his eyes. They're almost... sad. No, not almost. "You think I'm intense?"

"So intense you make me forget to breathe."

The flutter of breath on my forehead warns me he's drawing closer. I close my eyes as his lips brush my skin. I look at him when he responds.

"You're so intense, you make every cell in my body aware of your presence," he whispers, and his anger lowers even more. "You shine so bright, it almost hurts to look at you, like I'm staring directly at a beam of light." My throat tightens. He has to stop. He's going to make me cry, and I do not cry. "You're so beautiful, I feel as if I stare too long, I'll turn to stone."

"Stop."

We stare at each other in silence for two full beats before he speaks again. "Why?"

I don't know why. Words seem ludicrous when the feelings in your heart boil over. "I... Because we just met." Because I'm uncomfortable with praise, it's so foreign to me.

He shakes his head, and I don't know why.

Slowly, so slowly I don't realize what he's doing at first, he threads his fingers through my hair. The feeling's exquisite, sexy, relaxing, and comforting all at once. "When you touched the guns earlier, did you know right away which one fit in your palm? Did awareness strike you?"

The question surprises me almost as much as my answer. "Yes."

"There was a certain comfort in the touch, wasn't there? As if the others held power, but that one was designed just for you? Like someone waved a magic wand and crafted it to fit your palm?"

"Exactly. Yes, that's it."

He nods. My skin feels all prickly and hot. "That's how I felt when I saw you for the first time."

I brush off the compliment, because I'm squirming under his praise. "Cain, the first time you saw me, you looked as if you were bored by me."

His response is to lower his mouth and brush his lips across mine. I get the distinct feeling he's rejecting my comment, but I can't understand why, and then I forget what the comment or question even was. Because he's kissing me, our lips joined in a heated moment, and when Cain Master kisses me, the world fades to dust.

CHAPTER 14

Cain

I didn't mean for this to happen.

We've got an hour before my men will have their report ready for me.

I wasn't supposed to let her drive me to distraction, and I most definitely wasn't supposed to punish her.

Not now. Not here.

I love the way her eyelids flutter closed, and her hands wrap around my neck for support. I love the way she lets me hold her.

But we have a job to do, and I'm a shit teacher if I don't teach her how to use this gun.

I change my mind about waiting until tomorrow morning. "We need to practice."

"Right," she repeats. "Practice."

We pull away reluctantly.

She's a natural.

I want to wrap her up in my arms, carry her back to my room, and tie her to my bed.

No one would ever touch my Violet. She's mine.

What I'd do to her when I had her there...

But we have a job to do, and we don't have any more time to waste.

"You're really fucking good at this."

I love the way she flushes under my praise. "I have a good teacher."

"There are some things you can't teach. Some things that only come naturally."

I don't know if it's because she has years of training, because she's incredibly skilled at knife throwing, or because there's just something inside her that innately knows its way around weapons, but when she holds a gun and shoots, she does it as if she's had years of practice.

She doesn't trust me at first when she turns back around to shoot.

"Stop looking over your shoulder at me."

"I'm afraid you'll—do something to me again." She gives me a look halfway between a glare and a pout.

"Like spank you?" I love watching her squirm.

"Or—something."

I release a labored breath. "I will never, ever do anything to distract you when you're holding a gun." I shake my head. "Goddammit, woman, you think I wanna lose my balls?"

"Ah," she says, standing the way I showed her with her legs spread apart and knees slightly bent. "So I'm safe from being dominated when I hold a gun?"

I huff out a breath. "Yeah."

"I'll have to bring a gun with me to bed, then."

"Try it," I say dryly. "See how that works out for you."

She turns back to her target with a coy little smile. The first shot hits in the yellow ring, a shoulder strike for the human-shaped paper. "I meant that," she mutters. "I don't really want to kill anyone."

"If they're pulling a gun on you, yes, you do."

She doesn't reply, but her next shot strikes straight between the eyes.

"Good shot." I glance at my watch. Eight o'clock. "We have to go now. You'll join me here every morning at seven sharp."

I note the regret on her face when she lays her weapon down. "And lemme guess, no coming here without you even if I follow the rules?"

"If you come here without me, you're *not* following the rules."

"I'm not going to get any better if I don't practice."

"Trust me. We'll practice."

She draws in a breath and squares her shoulders. "I want to see you shoot."

"You want to see me shoot?"

Her pupils are dilated, and I realize… she's aroused.

No. She's on *fire*.

"It turns you on, doesn't it?"

"What?"

I feel a slow, lazy smile spread across my face. "All of it. Your spanking. The gun. Me, dominating you. Watching me hold a gun."

She swallows but doesn't look away. "Yes, Mr. Master. You could say that."

"Give me your knife, Violet."

Trembling, she bends and slips her knife out of its sheath.

"What about knives?" I hold the knife to the light. The blade glints like crystal.

"What… about them?" Her chest rises with a sharp intake of breath. I watch as her fingers come to rest on her hips, but her body's tense. Waiting.

"Have you ever played with knives?"

"Of course. All the time. The only way you learn to throw like I have is to—" Eyes wide, she swallows before she continues. "That's not the kind of knife play you have in mind, is it?"

"Not at all, sweet girl."

I brush the handle of the knife across her temple. Her eyes flutter closed, her lips parted. "Knife play can be intensely erotic. You would never want to play with a novice, but with the right person…if you have full trust…" My heartbeat races. "Stay still, Violet." I drag the edge of the knife along her jaw, a thin scraping that makes her skin white. She stands absolutely still. If she moved too quickly, she'd break skin. "Edge play takes you right to the very brink of danger and foreplay." I gently drag the knife from her jaw to her neck, the tiniest scrape of metal to skin. I lean in, my mouth against her ear. "But it intensifies *everything*."

Her eyes flutter open, and she licks her lips.

"You're good at that," she whispers.

"Good at what?"

"Intensifying everything."

I gently take the knife off her skin and hand it to her.

Brilliant violet eyes meet mine, unblinking. "I want to see you shoot. Please."

I step past her, my shoulder brushing hers, and my own need to claim this woman flares. I reach for my baby, the Ruger EC9. A striker-fired pistol with an easy trigger and immovable sights, it's my favorite for fast, meticulous shooting.

"Tell me where."

"Left shoulder."

Boom. Hit it.

"Midsection."

Boom. A hole tears straight through the abdominal region.

"Left ear."

Boom. Blast the ear straight fucking off.

"Right wrist."

Boom. Bingo.

"*Shit*. You're a perfect shot."

I shrug. "Some guys play video games. I relax at the target range."

"Why does this not surprise me?" I can't miss the unmistakable pride in her voice. It does strange things to me I don't know how to unpack. But we have to go.

I show her how to lock everything up. "Back at the house, you'll find clothes in your room. Wear something professional, so we get some answers."

I turn away before she can reply. I don't want to listen to any of her bullshit about not wanting the clothes I gave her. She'll wear the clothes.

My phone rings. Joe.

"Yeah?"

"Lottie called. No change. No word from Skylar, nothing at all."

I've never been a patient guy, and I sure as fuck am not one now. I hate that we're in a holding pattern until we can get more information.

"Thanks. You have that list of victims for us?"

"Yes, sir. Waiting for you in your office."

I head to my office to get the papers, then do a quick change myself so I look professional. Khakis, dress shoes, polo shirt. Someone knocks on the door.

"Come in."

The door creaks open, and I don't look up at first, fully consumed by the details I'm reading about the people we'll see today. When I get my hands on this motherfucker…

"Ahem."

I look up. I blink. I sit back in my chair and admire the stunning woman before me.

Violet's dressed in a white top and dress pants that show off her trim figure and gorgeous thighs. Her top fits her snugly, but drapes about her, somehow pulling off both professional and stunning all at once. Her hair is pulled back in a stylish braid, and she's wearing makeup that makes her cheeks brighter, her lips fuller, and her eyes... *God*, her eyes.

"Lock that door behind you and get over here."

A pleased smile tugs at her lips. "Is that an order, Mr. Master?"

Christ, I love it when she calls me that.

"It is."

She captures her lower lip between her teeth and casts her eyes down, but dutifully turns and locks the door behind her. When she turns back to me, her vivid eyes are even brighter.

"I literally have no idea how to fix this hair and makeup, so you can't muss it up." She thinks those hands on her hips somehow give her authority.

So cute.

I crook a finger at her. Her cheeks flush brighter.

"We have work to do."

"We do."

I tap the papers together on my desktop and push them to the side, shove away from my desk and walk around to the front. I meet her at the same time she reaches my desk, lift her, and place her on the edge.

I love the way she gasps and her hands fly to my shoulders to steady herself. I reach for her, embrace her, and tuck her against my chest.

"This is risky. You know that."

"I do."

I bend and kiss her, and for one brief moment in time, the world stops spinning.

"I could've worn the skirt," she says, as if to distract me from her stunning beauty. "But you can't run in a skirt, and you just never know…"

"You don't. Smart girl, we should be prepared."

"And I've been thinking."

"Yeah, baby?"

I love the way her eyes go soft when I call her *baby*.

"I don't think we should start with the victims. The only survivors don't remember what happened to them. We know that he went to Bubbles and Broomsticks, and we know that he has witnesses for every place he's gone."

"Exactly."

"But something occurred to me when I was getting changed just now."

I step back to look at her, so I can take her seriously.

"What's that?"

"The alibis for the times Derrick Dossier supposedly abducted his victims? They're detailed, but almost... *too* detailed. Here, look."

She takes out her phone and pulls up the notes app.

"August first. Flowers show up at Anita Charles' door. She goes on a date with a mysterious stranger and doesn't return. Her body's found two days later, but he has video evidence that he was shooting pool at the bar when she was supposedly abducted, then he was working the other hours. Like, he didn't even go home to get changed?"

"Odd."

"There's more."

I nod.

"Next up, Margaret Sellier. Flowers show up at her door. Like the others, same thing, goes on a date with a stranger and doesn't return. That time, he was with three buddies fishing in Panama, and couldn't possibly have kidnapped anyone, yet..."

Her voice trails off. I wait for her to finish.

"Yet there's actual DNA evidence to prove it was him."

I shake my head. "That doesn't make sense."

"We don't know who struck us yesterday in the car, but we do know that whoever this person or persons are, they're specifically targeting people who..." She flushes pink. "Who mean something to *you*. But... you didn't know me until yesterday."

I can't tell her that isn't true. She'd run.

No one knew she mattered to me.

"I say we go back to the bar. I say we bait him. He has bartenders there that slip roofies in drinks for him so he can do his thing, right? At least the one we already took care of."

"Right."

"Then use me as bait."

"No *fucking* way."

My hands have risen to her shoulders, and she gently pushes them down to rest on her thighs.

"Yes. I can go in and pretend I'm asking more questions, searching for more answers. I'll be a sitting duck drawing him out, and the entire time, we'll have your team keep looking to see what they can find. He's already tried to get me anyway; we'll just make it that much easier for us to find him."

"*No.* And if you try to do it on your own, I swear to God, Violet—"

"I know, I know, you'll tie me up, right?"

I curse under my breath, and she waves me off.

"He's watching us. You know he is. You know he was at my place and he knows I'm here now, he has to, if his motive is to get the people that matter to you."

I shake my head. I hate that my sister's missing. I hate that she's in danger. But there has to be another way.

Holding my gaze, her voice softens. She takes one of my hands from her thigh and turns it around so she cups it in two of her own. "We have to do something."

My throat feels tight. I nod. "Yeah."

"We have to find out who he is. Let's sit with your team and piece together what we have. But I really think our time's better spent at the bar than here or questioning those poor survivors who were traumatized anyway."

I cringe. "Right."

Her eyes harden. "I looked at the pictures of the victims. I've made connections. And I saw some things I never, ever want to see again." She cringes. "I won't tell you details because of Skylar, but believe me, we need to stop this guy."

"Agreed." I pull away from her with reluctance. "Let's go."

We're ten minutes out. I love the way she's hyperfocused and aware, her back ramrod straight as she sits next to me in the truck.

"Some people like pretty cars," she says softly, fingering the leather details on the interior of my truck. "Some like race cars or convertibles or expensive, luxury cars. I mean, your Lamborghini's nice," she says with a shrug, in the same tone of voice one might say, *I mean, it'll do.*

I feel the corners of my lips quirk up. *It'll do.* "But you?"

She sighs contentedly and runs her hands palms down over the leather-clad dash. "If I could, I would spread my legs for this truck and fuck it good and hard, cowgirl style."

I nearly hit the curb and catch myself just in time. "My God, woman. There's a visual I won't forget. What do you love about trucks?"

With a contented sigh, still running her hands over the leather, she grows meditative. "I like dangerous, powerful things. Your pit bulls, for instance. Some see nothing but a vicious, lethal dog. I see strength and loyalty, and they're so beautiful to me I could cry. I love how when you sit in a truck like this, you're above everyone else."

"On top of the world," I say softly. Violet gets it.

She moves closer to me, our bodies flush against each other in the cab. "I've always loved powerful, dangerous things." Her fingers trail down my bicep, tracing the edges of muscles and veins. "Makes me feel... protected, I guess, but at the same time... not safe at all." With what I know about her background, I understand. She sighs. "That doesn't make sense."

"It makes perfect sense."

I accelerate when we get on the on ramp. Her grip on my arm tightens.

We're five minutes out.

My phone rings. Joe. I hit the button on the steering wheel so we can both hear.

"Yeah?"

"I've got Derrick Dossier on the line for you."

CHAPTER 15

Violet

If looks could kill, his phone would be incinerated right about now. I cringe at the latent threat in his voice.

"I want everyone in surveillance on this call."

"On it, sir."

I watch as he releases a breath. "Connect the call." There's a series of clicks. "Cain Master speaking."

"Ahhh, Mr. Master. We meet again." I shiver at the unpleasant sound of Dossier's voice. Some voices are musical, almost lyrical. Others are neutral. Dossier's makes the hairs on the back of my neck stand up. "You don't remember me, do you?"

Cain glances at me. Someone he does know, or should know, as we suspected.

"No. Where's my sister?"

"Settle down, Mr. Master. I have your sister right here."

Cain's shaking with anger, but I can tell he's relieved as well.

Skylar's alive. I exhale and reach my fingers to his knee. I give him a reassuring squeeze.

"Why don't you put her on the phone." His tone is deceptively calm. He's a raging inferno, ready to annihilate. I'm not even the one he's angry at, and his roiling fury has me trembling.

"Now, now, Mr. Master, no need to be hasty. Relax. Skylar and I are having a brilliant time, aren't we?"

Do I detect an accent? If there is one, it's faint.

"Cain!" A young female voice sounds frantic on the other line. "It's a setup. Don't come!" Like that would stop him. An armed squad paired with a bomb threat wouldn't stop him.

There's a scuffling noise then the sound of a thump and a muffled cry.

"If you hurt her, I'll kill you." I feel as if actual fire shoots from Cain's eyes.

"That's what you like to do, isn't it? Kill people just for the hell of it, don't you? You don't care who you kill. You don't care if people have family. The ends always justify the means with you, don't they?"

Cain doesn't respond but goes deadly calm.

His eyes flick to mine and I can't quite read him.

"What do you want?"

"You can't give me what I want, Master." Oh, the irony of him calling Cain Master. "So I'll do what you do oh so well. I'll take what's mine."

"If you—"

The line goes dead. He grabs the phone, curses, and it looks like he's going to whip it right out the window. I grab his arm. "Stop! You'll need that if he calls you again. I know, I want to break things, too."

The truck comes to a rumbling stop at the side of the road. He tosses it into park and buries his head in his hands. Shoulders heaving, I wonder at first if he's crying. The thought terrifies me.

Gently, I reach a hand to his shoulder. He's breathing heavily, his body tense like a bowstring pulled too tightly. He's going to snap.

"We'll find her," I tell him, determined. "I don't care what it takes. We'll find him."

When he lifts his head, his eyes are too bright, but he hasn't cried. Still, it breaks my heart to see him so tortured.

"He's right, Violet. I did kill, and I have no regrets. I did it for my country. For my soldiers at arms."

I read his files. I know what he did, what he's capable of. But I don't see a bad man. No. Only a good man would feel the weight of his actions the way Cain does. Only a good man would lay down life and limb for the people he loves. He's loyal to his very core.

I gentle my voice. "One thing at a time. Let's go over what he said. Did your team get anything at all?"

The call was too brief, all ability to track expertly blocked.

"Okay, alright, so let's put our heads together. He says you know him. How would you know him?"

"Must've been when I served in the military."

"In France?"

He gives me a short nod. "Yeah."

"Tell me what happened there. Would anyone have reason to want to kill you?"

"*Lots* of people want to kill me. Fucking dozens. I was in charge of protecting the U.S. Embassy. It came to my knowledge there was going to be an attack, so I acted." He blows out a breath. "If I had it to do over again, I would behave differently, but honest to God…" His voice trails off, and he shakes his head. "I did what I thought was best at the time." He glances at the clock on the dash. "I don't have time to go into detail."

"Summary, please. I need to know."

"Fine. The short version. We were subject to a hostile militia attack at our embassy access points. They began at night and went into the day. The attacks were unprovoked and considered an act of war and had to be stopped or many, many more would've died. The attacks focused on the arrival of American diplomats who'd come to the Embassy to sign an agreement with the U.N., but the agreement had a direct impact on weapons sales across the Mediterranean."

I nod. Following.

"It was one attack after another. Since we were attacked, we sent an airstrike, which killed dozens. So when I got word the militia was preparing for a counterattack, I sent our men to ward that off." His lips thin. "Their initial attacks cost us twenty million in fire damage, and we lost two dozen of our soldiers, not to mention dozens of innocents. I couldn't let more devastation happen."

"Of course not," I say, squeezing his knee. I hate that he bears this burden, to this day.

"So we attacked them before their counter strike, and we killed the entire militia. It's the worst memory I have, and one I wish I could erase forever."

"I understand. I have a few like that myself."

We're only a few blocks away from the bar now.

"There are ways of erasing bad memories," I say gently.

He reaches for my fingers and gives my hand a little squeeze. "Yeah? How?"

"You replace them with new ones."

We drive by the business section of town, where the office parks are lined up near restaurants and retail shops. Something flashes by my window, and suddenly, a spark fuses in my brain and I have the answer, with lightning clarity.

I *know*.

"Stop!"

The truck comes to a screeching halt as he yanks the steering wheel to the right and pulls to the side of the road. "What is it?"

"The flowers. Oh, God, Cain, the flowers. You said you think this guy has history in France, right?"

"Yes."

"The flowers he's been sending. The beautiful purplish-blue flowers, those are irises, right? He puts them next to the baby's breath."

He's staring at me now with so much intensity, I feel hot under the glare. "Yes?"

"The iris is the national flower of France. Baby's breath represents innocence, doesn't it?"

He nods.

"Criminals who leave clues think they're clever, that they can outsmart the police. Most of them are narcissists. He did this out of pride, to taunt us."

"Did *what*?" He's clearly running out of patience.

I talk faster. "The fleur-de-lis emblem, the one with the flower and leaves? French symbol. *Fleur-de-*

lis. He's taken every single woman right here in Salem, the *very same* city with the Fleur-de-lis Memorial."

His phone rings again as he pulls back out into the intersection. *Joe.*

"Boss, we found something we think you need to know."

"Don't keep me waiting."

"You ordered us to find the names of the people killed in the counterattack of the Embassy to see if anyone was connected to Dossier. We found none by the name of Dossier, sir. We did, however, find a *Dozier.* Actually, two. Twins. One was killed, the survivor moved to America. We found him, and he fits the profile of the man they've suspected of being behind these attacks."

I suddenly feel cold. "Could... someone from another country become a police officer here in the States?"

"Depends on the state but yes, many departments will allow it."

"So the former police officer that's suspected in the abductions and rape cases... could've been the same man you fought overseas... especially if he fudged his age here in the U.S."

"Yes."

I think this over. "Cain. Dozier's French for willow... it's the surname for someone who lived near a plantation of willows... if you killed his twin..." I smack my forehead. "Skip the bar, we can't go there. We have to go to the Salem Willows, it's where the Fleur-de-lis Memorial is!" My heart races with excitement. We've had a breakthrough. "It's a hunch, but my hunches are very, very good."

"Don't get too excited. He likely laid this out precisely so we'd find him. Remember, Skylar said it was a setup."

The Salem Willows Park is thirty-five acres along the ocean, named because of the white willow trees planted along the walkways to offer shade. The long, graceful branches nearly graze the ground they've grown so long, and on warm summer days like today, it's not unusual to find families strolling along the paths, ice cream cones in hand, or bike riders whizzing past on two wheels. The rocky beach borders large, grassy fields, where people often picnic or play frisbee.

Around the Willows, though, are several residential houses, apartment complexes and rentals, video arcades and vendors selling carnival food and treats.

The Fleur-de-lis Memorial stands in the center of Salem Willows Park, only steps away from the main attractions.

When we arrive, the park is teeming with people, dogs, and bicyclists. We park the truck at the edge and move quickly to the Fleur-de-lis.

My skin prickles.

Here. He's here.

They're here. I know they are.

Cain whips his head around, scouring the passersby, but it's hard to tell even where to begin.

"Too many people here," he mutters. "Too many goddamn civilians. We'll have to find them and isolate them."

A shiver skates down my spine. I've read what he does to them when he has them alone. "But first we have to find them."

When we draw near to the Fleur-de-lis, I don't see anything that can lead us to where Dossier's got Skylar.

We walk up and down the paths, intent on finding details or something that would give us a clue.

Near the arcade, something purple catches my eye.

"Cain." I point wordlessly, as my stomach churns with acid. Bordering the entrance to the arcade are gorgeous purple irises in full bloom.

"They usually bloom earlier in the year," I say to Cain, shaking my head. "But spring was late with the cold weather, and they've bloomed later than usual." He exhales as I continue, "He used those flowers because he wants you to find him."

His hand takes mine as we walk side by side. "You ready for this?" Cain asks.

"The man tried to attack me. He used intimidation tactics and hurt me. He came after your sister and other innocent women and did the very worst things he could have. Am I ready for this?" I huff out a mirthless laugh. "I may fight you off so I can kill him myself."

My breathing hitches when he tugs me a little closer to him and says in a low voice laced with approval, "That's my girl. We'll fight him. We'll rescue Skylar. And then we'll kill him."

"They do call you the executioner. I hope you live up to the name." I love the way his eyes light up, even as a mask of fury and resolve etches lines around his eyes.

"You do know how to flirt with a guy, don't you?"

"Not in the slightest. But with you, I'm learning."

We move gracefully. As one.

"We'll go into the arcade. See what we can find. I texted Joe and my surveillance team, they're getting back to me with specs on the arcade's layout."

It's dim and hot in the arcade. Skee ball flanks one wall, across from air hockey machines and foosball tables. Large, clunky machines spit out coins and tickets, and everywhere we turn, I see flashing lights. I can hardly hear myself think in here with the bells and whistles and loud, raucous music.

Cain says something to me, but I can hardly hear him. I shake my head to tell him I can't hear him. He lifts his phone. He's got the arcade blueprint.

Two floors. The first houses video games, skee ball, and the table games, but upstairs are the classic games, virtual reality, and funhouse. Behind the funhouse are storage rooms and a small studio apartment.

They could be anywhere.

According to this map, the stairs are to the left of the foosball tables. I reach for his hand so we don't get separated in the crush of people. I locate the dimly lit back stairs. He goes ahead of me but reaches his hand behind him so we don't let go.

The noise increases as we go upstairs. At first, my heart beats faster at the sound of a scream, but at the top of the stairs I see a macabre Halloween game with a screaming banshee. A few teens are laughing and playing, racking up points for every scream the banshee shouts. A few feet away, my body's tall and distorted in the funhouse mirror, and Cain's looks oddly frightening with a twisted clown's face staring at us.

"I hate arcades," I mutter to myself. "I fucking hate them."

I once got lost in an arcade as a child and never forgot it. They're easy to get lost in. Cain doesn't know how much it means to me that he's holding my damn hand.

I jump when one of the teens hits the jackpot, the screaming banshee's wails pitching louder and louder. Cain frowns, his eyes narrowed. Here, right behind these walls, are the storage rooms and studio apartment, likely designed for the owners to live in or rent.

"Those fucking screams don't help," I mutter. His body goes rigid.

"Christ, Violet. That isn't the machine," he says. I look wildly back to see the teens have gone, the game is back to the "start" menu, but the screams haven't stopped. A chill runs down my spine.

"Through here," I say, pointing a finger at the break room door. "In here."

It's locked, but that doesn't stop him. It's an old wooden door that opens inward, and the locks look flimsy. A perfect setup. "Back up."

The guy's a human bulldozer, larger than any other human I've ever met, and he knows how to use his body. He lets loose with a roundhouse kick, followed by a shoulder ram. The door whines and cracks. Another kick, shoulder, kick, shoulder. The door splinters and breaks. I help him kick the broken wood aside, half expecting someone to attack, but no one comes at us at first.

He steps through, and I follow behind him. "Be careful, Violet." Like him, I expect someone to attack at any moment. No one comes. My spine straightens at another scream, louder this time, and it's not coming from behind us but in front of us.

In seconds, I've got a knife in each hand, and he's cocked his gun. I wish I was experienced enough to have one too, but I'll get there. The knives are only my backup. My body's my main weapon.

There's no movement ahead of us or around us. I don't look at Cain, both of us focused. It's a small room that leads into another, the curtains and shades drawn tight so the room's darkened. A yellowed, bare bulb hangs from the entryway, throwing off a weak glow. Broken arcade games surround both sides, some with wires hanging out, others with cracked screens, the machines tilted on their sides like discarded gaming carcasses. I shiver. There's something eerie about them.

Another scream. My heart beats so fast I feel nauseous. Cain breaks through the rubble and runs. For the huge guy he is, he runs *fast*. I run behind him, panting to keep up, and we come to another doorway, this one with no door. This room must've been part of a haunted house or something similar back in the day. Discarded party decorations litter the floor. We enter the room; it's lined with boxes, so dark it's hard to see a damn thing.

A wall of stench hits my nostrils, and I cover my mouth and nose. The unmistakable scent of body odor, sweat, and sex lingers in the air. My mouth waters with the need to vomit, and bile burns the back of my throat, but I have to keep my head on straight. I can't lose my shit now.

Cain's boots crunch on broken glass as another scream tears through the quiet.

Cain sees them before I do. I know this the second he whips out his gun and aims. "You motherfucker. Put the light on, Vi. I want to see the life leave his eyes when I kill him."

Him. One. There's only one? He stands directly in front of me so I can't see a damn thing.

I look around frantically for a light switch and finally see one behind a stack of boxes. I lean in and flick it on. The room lights up, revealing a bulky guy not much older than I am wearing an eye patch, his long black hair covering his face like a shroud. He grins like he's just won the lottery. Beside him tied to the bed lies a young woman in a tank top and nothing else, her body laced with lacerations and angry red welts.

"Cain," she says in a tearful voice. "I told you not to come, I don't want you to get hurt."

"Ahh, Mr. Master. I see you—"

"Get down and cover."

I take a split second to process the command he snaps out before I drop to my knees and cover my ears, the cold metal of my knives on either side framing my face. One gunshot, two, a third I feel straight in my belly, and Dossier's body falls to the floor heavily. He screams, grabbing his arm.

"Secure Skylar, Violet. Leave him to me."

"Cain!" I stare in surprise as a second man enters the room who looks remarkably like Dossier. He brandishes a gun in the doorway. I don't think, but fling my knife with perfect precision directly at him. It strikes his belly as gunshots erupt. He falls to the floor, his face a mask of fury as he lunges for me. I roll and duck as he strikes out, dodging every attempt to hit me.

I have a second knife I whip at his leg. It hits precisely above his knee. He grabs at the knife, howling with rage, just as a gunshot hits his shoulder. Another one hits him in his other shoulder. I look up to see Cain staring down at him, his gun still smoking.

I know he's a perfect shot. He didn't aim to kill. He's here to capture. The killing will be a different story.

Dossier's bleeding behind him, his hand on his head as blood drips down his fingers.

Cain pulls out his phone and makes a call.

"Upper room. They're both alive, but not for long so fucking *move*."

"You bastard! You think this is over?" Dossier spits blood and spittle on the ground in front of him.

"Oh, no," Cain says with that smile that chills me to the bone. "Nowhere close to over." He falls to one knee beside Dossier. "Violet, you secure the other asshole."

"Happily." I yank my knife from the guy's leg and hold it to his temple. "You hurt innocent women. If you move, I'll slice your throat." My hand shakes with the effort of holding myself back.

"You tried to kill my brother in Paris," Dossier shouts. "You left him for dead. You son of a bitch, so proud of yourself."

"I defended my country. You kidnapped and raped innocent women," Cain says. I turn to look as Cain reaches over and squeezes his shoulder. Blood pours out of the wound and Dossier screams like a dying animal. "We'll both burn in hell for what we've done, but not until I'm good and ready to let you go."

Twins. The one supposedly killed wasn't dead after all. It all makes sense.

Dossier and his brother worked in tandem, one with an obvious alibi while the other kidnapped their victims. I'd bet good money both raped them. DNA evidence proved Dossier was the perpetrator because he was. Twin DNA is often so close it's indistinguishable.

Now that it's clear, I don't know how we missed it before. Twins. Fucking *twins*.

I scream when something strikes my back, pain radiating from my spine to my neck. I grab at my back and feel something wet and sticky. I look in disbelief at my hand covered in blood.

He sliced me with my own damn knife, but not very well. It grazed my skin but didn't stick.

"You son of a bitch." Cain lands a vicious kick to the Dossier he's got, then another and another until he slumps onto the floor. He swivels and lands a vicious kick to the other's belly. Blood spurts to the floor, and before he can recover, Cain hammers an uppercut to his abdomen with his right hand, then a jab to his jaw with his left, a brutal combination that leaves the other Dossier wheezing as he collapses again.

"You took my sister." Cain strikes him again, his fist like an anvil. "You raped innocent women." Dossier number two yanks his arms up to cover his face and openly cries, his tears mingled with blood, but I feel no sympathy. I want to see him suffer. I want to see him cry. "You dared to hurt *my woman.*" The next punch breaks bone. Dossier number two is a human punching bag and Cain has hit his rhythm, punching until he's unconscious.

"Cain!" I damn near risk my life and grab at his arm as he rears back to deliver what will no doubt be the blow that kills Dossier. The latent power in his arm sizzles through me, and I almost release him, but make myself hold fast. "While this is highly entertaining, you have to stop." He's panting with the exertion, sweat dripping down his face. I gentle my voice. "You have to stop, Cain. You have to leave something for us to interrogate."

The other one lunges at me, and I step out of the way just in time.

"Right." Cain faces the other Dossier, baring his teeth. "You piece of shit. You'll get a taste of the same fucking medicine."

"Cain," I say pleadingly. "Let me?"

He reaches down with a sickening smile and grabs Dossier by the hair. "Have at it, baby."

I swivel and give him a roundhouse kick. I hit him as hard as I can. He doubles over, grabbing his stomach. I knee him in the back and he falls to the floor. "You hurt his sister. You hurt innocent women. You broke into my house, and you made my man *bleed.*" I puncture every word with another jab, strike, and kick until he's whimpering and begging for mercy. It hasn't even begun to satisfy my thirst for violence when Cain speaks.

"Alright, Violet," Cain says, with unmistakable pride in his voice that makes my chest swell.

"He deserves more than that."

"And I'll make sure he gets what he deserves."

I look into Cain's eyes and reach my hand up to cup his jaw. His icy blue gaze locks with mine. "*Promise* me."

Gently extracting my hand from his face, he kisses each bloodied fingertip, one by one. "I promise you, sweetheart. I'll make them pay. Both of them."

A thrill of arousal races through me.

I might love this monster of a man.

Satisfied, I look around the room and see wires hanging out of a broken video game. I slice them with one of my knives, then tie both men at their ankles and wrists so I can get to Skylar.

Cain and I unfasten her and lead her off the dirty bed, grabbing a sheet to wrap around her waist. She trembles but walks beside me.

"Are you alright?" I ask her.

She looks away and doesn't answer at first, then finally nods. "I am now."

I walk back to the bed while Cain drags both men to it. He hauls one up like he's a sack of potatoes and tosses him unceremoniously on the bed. The guy whimpers. He takes the second, hog-tied and immobile, and tosses him beside his brother. Even though they're beaten beyond recognition and tied fast, he has me hold both men at gunpoint while he makes the call.

I don't even want to think about what he'll do to them when he brings them back to his place. I haven't even begun to explore the many rooms he has at his home, but something tells me the target range isn't the only soundproof room in the house. And I remember what I've read about his methods.

These men will wish we'd killed them here.

Skylar stares at me with large, frightened eyes.

"Who are you?" Her voice is wobbly, broken. My heart splinters. I don't even want to think about what she's been through.

I give her a gentle smile. "My name's Violet."

Skylar gives me a tentative smile back, through her obvious pain. "That's a beautiful name."

CHAPTER SIXTEEN

Violet

It's late into the night. Darkness settles over the house on the hill, as the sun set hours ago. Skylar's soundly sleeping in one of the guest rooms on the main floor, sedated by the doctor. She needs rest now more than anything.

Cain has her heavily guarded. I didn't think I liked Cain's straightlaced bodyguard the day I came here. Now I've never been so happy to see him.

Today, we brought down the men responsible for the abductions and rapes. Under Cain's... questioning, one might call it... we got full confessions. And I was right about them working in tandem. We have much to unpack, and will, but the greatest threat is over.

Cain takes on the task of telling his team all that happened, and instructs me to call Candi. "Then go to your room. Relax and get some rest. I'll come see you when I'm through down here." I know without him telling me that he'll be "through down there" when his men lay twin bodies in shallow graves. I'm not upset by this. I'd be disappointed with anything less.

I'm not surprised there are two armed men on either side of my door when I arrive at the guest room. We have to make sure neither Dossier was in league with anyone. We don't know for sure yet that this was the end of the attacks.

So when I'm finally settled in, I call Candi and alert her that we've found the men responsible for Cain's sister's abduction, but they were killed.

Candi's voice is weary when she asks, "Do I want to know the rest of this story, babe?"

"No, Candi. You don't."

"Are you safe?"

My answer's no more certain now than it was the last time she asked me. Once again, I lie to my best friend. "Yeah. I'm safe."

"Violet… be careful. Cain Master is a dangerous, *dangerous* man. I don't like that you're involved with him. I don't like it at *all*."

I don't know how to tell her the fact that he's a dangerous man might be what draws me to him the most.

She takes my statement and tells me she'll come for a full report in the morning. I look forward to it. Somehow, seeing my best friend here might make this all seem real. My two worlds will collide… but it's time.

I don't want to see anyone else right now and definitely don't feel like talking to anyone, so I settle into my room for the night. I've showered and put on pajamas. I played mindless games on my phone. I'm too wired to settle down.

I get up and go to the walk-in closet. I finger the clothes, stroke the fine fabrics, and marvel at the sheer volume of luxury. They're gorgeous, every single one of them, and he says they're all for me. I'm too tired to try anything on just now, but when I dressed earlier, everything I tried fit me perfectly.

And the *shoes...* good God, the shoes alone could buy me a townhouse right here by the ocean. Heels and flats, sandals and boots, an array of colors and fabrics that would be the envy of any shoe aficionado.

Why?

How long does he think I'll stay?

It's a little unsettling, if I'm honest.

What's the catch?

And does it matter? I'm here for a reason, and I won't leave until I've done what I came for.

But now I make myself face the truth I've been avoiding.

I want to see Cain. I want to touch him, feel him.

And I want much, much more than the kiss I got last night.

After what we've been through…

I hear heavy footsteps outside my door, and the low rumble of a voice that can only be him. I sit up in bed, my heart racing, as he knocks just before the door opens. He stands in the doorway, the light from the hall casting him in shadow, but I know it's him.

"No one fills a doorframe like *that*."

He turns his head as if just realizing there's a doorframe there.

I can hear the humor in his voice when he responds, "No one fills a bed like *that*."

I look around me at the cavernous bed. "I'm *hardly* filling it." I give him a little pout. "There's plenty of room still here."

The door shuts with an audible *bang*.

I jump. Liquid heat pools between my legs. I forget to breathe.

"Are the guards still there?" My whole being is filled with wanting.

He prowls closer to me, the shadows falling behind him. "Of course not. I told them to go because I'm here now."

I briefly close my eyes to quell the rise of emotion. He told the guards to go because *I'm safe with him.*

I open my eyes. As he draws nearer, he never takes his eyes from mine. The shadow's behind him now, and the pale yellow light from the bedside table illuminates his features.

His ruggedly masculine face, lined with weariness, is speckled with blood, his jaw covered in thick black stubble, but I've never seen anyone so beautiful in my life. His strong features hold inherent masculinity, underscored by the harsh slash of his mouth softened by full lips. When I first met him, I wondered if he could pull a sword out of a stone or bare his teeth and show me his fangs. I almost laughed at myself, at my imagination.

Now, I know he could do that and more. So much more.

He locks me in the power of his gaze. His eyes show the same raging fury and power they did when I first saw him. Only now, I see that the simmering anger only boils at the surface. It will take me years to unearth what lies beneath.

I can wait.

He sighs wearily when he reaches the bed. Bending to grasp the edge of his T-shirt, he lifts it up over his body, the fabric bunching and swaying before he tosses it to the side. I briefly wonder if his broad shoulders ever bow under the weight of what he carries.

I wonder if he'll ever share that burden.

I let my gaze rove lazily over his chest, the smattering of dark, coarse hair, defined abs, and a thin chain with dog tags. When he sees me looking at them, he lifts them off and places them gently on the bed. That's a story for another day then.

"You alright?" he asks, his voice a low rumble that sets my nerves on fire.

I shake my head. "No. You?"

"No." He gives me a slow, lazy smile. "I need a shower, baby. So fucking bad. Think you can help me?"

I love it when he calls me baby.

I'm on my feet before I realize what I'm doing. My hands shake when I reach for his belt. I unfasten the clasp and slide it through the loops, then lay it on the side of the bed. He watches me, his hands on his hips, as I reach for the button of his jeans and slide to my knees in front of him. With slow precision, I remove his pants, my breath catching as I tug them down his legs. He steps first one foot out, then the other, and his pants join his tee on the floor.

I can see the outline of his erection through his boxers. Like everything about him, it's larger than life. I lick my lips and swallow. I imagine what it would be like to take him in my mouth, to please him. I've never done that for anyone before, but I want to for him.

I don't know why, but I'm overcome with emotion. Maybe it's because I've been through so much in such a short time. Maybe because I know now that we've found his sister and she's safe, it's time to move on to the job I know I have to do.

Or maybe it's because I know I want him and can't bear the thought he doesn't want me the way I do him. Does he? I close my eyes and lay my cheek against his thigh. The dark, prickly hair scratches my cheek, as his hand comes to the back of my head and holds me there.

We don't speak. I kneel between his legs, my arms wrapped around him. I need a moment, and somehow, he knows that. He gives it to me before he bends, then kneels in front of me. Holds me. Right there on the floor, nearly naked, he tugs me onto his lap so my legs wrap around him to straddle his waist.

My body kindles with my need for him, his length pressed up against my panties. He wraps his fingers around the back of my neck and tugs me closer to him. My eyes meet his, and I know he's going to kiss me.

He rises with me in his arms, my legs still tucked around him, then lays me on the bed. His hands tangle in my hair and he holds my mouth to his but I need no persuasion. His huge, muscular frame pins me to the bed. I release a breath he swallows and makes his own. My breasts heave, pressed tight against his unyielding chest, and liquid heat cascades between my legs. His tongue licks mine, drawing an inhuman moan from me.

"I want you, Violet. All of you."

I nod dumbly, ready to give him anything and everything he wants. Right now, I want his hands and mouth and cock and body joined with mine in every possible combination. I want to kiss and lick and worship his body.

I want to bring him pleasure and surrender to bliss.

I want *everything.*

His hand cups my breast, and I whimper with the sudden flare of need that makes me tremble. His thumb flicks over my nipple. I nearly come.

"Cain," I whisper on a choked breath, so desperate to be closer to him I can't speak.

Silently, he lowers his mouth to my breast and licks the hardened nipple. A spasm of pleasure ripples through me so hard my hips jerk upward. He suckles again. My clit throbs on the edge of release. "*Fuuuccck,* baby," he growls in my ear. "I need to taste you."

I'm a ragdoll to his touch, pliable and boneless, as he arranges me on the bed and drops to his knees. When he looks at me, my heart turns over in my chest. I hold my breath as he parts my knees like he's worshipping me, the sexiest damn thing I've ever seen. He kisses the inside of my thigh, as he slides his thumb along my panty-clad slit. My hips buck. My pulse races. He kisses my right thigh. I'm still gasping for breath when he tugs my panties down and releases a deep, masculine groan I feel straight between my legs.

Holding my thighs in his big, very capable hands, he spreads them further apart. Exposing me. His eyes meet mine with a burning insolence, as if daring me to turn away now. I couldn't if I tried. My choice was made when he stepped through that door.

No. My choice was made the day I came here.

His eyes burning into me, he slowly lowers his mouth. He lazily drags his tongue along my swollen, throbbing clit, again and again. I cry out, my hips jerk. A moan of ecstasy slips through my lips, my palms flat on the bed on either side of me to keep me from flying away. My body quivers on the edge of ecstasy, the first spasm of orgasm echoing through me. He pumps his fingers in me. I shatter.

I can't breathe, I can't think, as my body bucks under the pressure of my climax. I come so hard, so many times, his heavy body atop mine, his length pressed between my legs. I scream his name until I'm hoarse.

Still riding the waves of ecstasy, I feel his breath in my ear before he says in a ragged voice, "I want to be in you when you come again. I want to feel you climax with me."

"Again? I'll die." I grab the back of his neck, pull him to me, and slam my mouth on his. "Bring it."

His low, masculine chuckle sends a spasm of pleasure straight through me. "I promise you, baby. I'll make it worth it. Over. And over. And over again." He kisses my cheek while he holds me, his length throbbing along with my pulse. A deep sense of peace invades my senses. I feel like I belong here. I know I can trust him.

Hypnotized by his touch, I surrender to him. I've never surrendered to anyone in my life.

This feels so right.

I study his face unhurriedly, each perfect, harsh, beautifully masculine detail. I love the way he looks at me hungrily, the way his muscles tighten, as if he's holding himself back.

"Make love to me, Cain."

His weight flush against me, he moves with determination, braces himself over me, and lines himself up between my legs. Then my wrists are trapped in his big, unyielding hands, as he puts his lips on mine.

He thrusts. I scream out loud. He stills.

"Don't," I pant. "Don't stop. *Please.*"

He skims a hand down my side as he thrusts again and again, gliding in and out of my slick heat in a perfect rhythm. Every thrust undoes me, every bolt of blissful pleasure makes me whole again. He swells inside me, but I take him. Each thrust sends sparks of pleasure rolling through me until I can't hold myself back any longer.

He releases a deep, masculine moan so ragged and raw, I lose myself to bliss and join him in ecstasy.

Seconds, moments, hours later, I'm still tangled in his taut limbs. He rolls over and tucks me to his chest. I can't move. I can't even open my eyes. It's a wonder to me he even has the strength to lace his fingers through my hair, and yet he does.

"I'm on birth control," I say on a sigh, half dead.

"Your timing's impeccable," he says with another one of those manly chuckles I wish I could record and play in an endless loop. I'd pay money to hear that again.

"I'm good like that. You still need to shower?"

"No, baby. I don't need anything now."

CHAPTER 16

Violet

"Eyes on the target. Do *not* take your eyes off the target."

"If I take my eyes off the target, do I get—"

"Don't try me, woman."

I grin as I pull the trigger.

Boom.

Boom.

Boom.

Three perfect shots right where I aimed.

Yes.

I feel his heat behind me before I see him, warm hands on my hips. I close my eyes when he kisses my cheek.

"I've never seen anyone learn how to hit a mark so quickly."

Oh yeah? I want to ask him. What do you call this?

I haven't returned to my apartment. I'm here for a reason, and I'm not leaving now until I've fulfilled my job. Until my mission's complete.

At least that's what I tell myself.

I feel the cool of his dog tags on my neck, and mentally imagine they kiss my scars. I'm feeling a bit sentimental today.

Skylar's home safe, and Cain has his answers.

Now it's my turn.

Unearthing who he is—who *I* am—is as much a mystery as finding Skylar's kidnapper.

"Eyes on the target, baby," he repeats. His much larger hands cover mine.

We stand as one.

We breathe as one.

Pull the trigger as one.

The blast of the gun reverberates through me, but we brace for the kickback together.

We shoot a perfect bullseye.

CHAPTER 17

Cain

THE END of the Dossier twins is the end of the terror inflicted on the innocent women of Salem.

Skylar needs time and some TLC, but I make sure she has it. She's bonded with Violet, and sometimes I don't know who appreciates that more. They become fast friends.

I'm glad.

It gives me a reason to keep her here.

I'd put a ring on her finger if it were up to me.

Not now. Not yet. My caged bird will fly if I try to hold her in captivity.

But now it's time…

I can help her find her parents' killers, and I will help her seek the vengeance she craves. I know I have what she wants.

What she doesn't know yet is how badly I want *her.* All of her. Completely, irrevocably… forever.

One day after target practice, I ask her to come up to my office. When she walks in the door, my heart does a somersault. I lean against the edge of my desk and beckon to her.

"Come here, baby."

I love that look she gets when I call her to me. Part daring, part hopeful, and all kinds of aroused.

When she reaches me, I run my hand up and down her back slowly, until she breathes a little freer and she lays her head on my shoulder. She fits right here, within my arms. She belongs here.

The office is so quiet, my words hang heavily between us.

"Candi says we've had nothing but quiet here in Salem. The biggest issue is keeping the teens from toilet papering the House of the Seven Gables on Halloween."

"I could stop them."

She snorts. "I bet you could, but you've got bigger fish to fry, don't you?"

I do. I run my hands along her shoulders, then down her slim waist to rest on her hips.

"You want to find your parents' killers, Violet?"

I watch her shoulders rise as she inhales, then fall as she lets her breath out. "I do, Cain. More than anything in the world."

Anything in the world.

I trace my fingers along her spine. "You helped me find my sister."

"Yes."

"And that, sweetheart, was your first task for me."

She nods, as I slowly turn us so she's now leaning against the desk and extend the trajectory of my touch. Past her back. Up her shoulders. Over her collarbone, then lower to where her ass meets the desk.

"But I want more than your work, Violet."

I place a gentle kiss on her neck, then open my mouth and suck in her damp, sweet flesh. I watch her knuckles whiten on the edge of the desk.

"What do you want from me?"

I place my hands on either side of her. My frame dwarfs hers. "I want *you*."

A slow blink as she absorbs my words.

"Me?"

"You. *All of you.* Carte blanche to do whatever I want to you, whenever I want to. Anytime, anywhere."

Her eyelids flutter closed, like a little bird's, her words a mere whisper. "I have the distinct feeling I'd... both hate and love every minute of what you'd do to me."

"Love and hate are so irrevocably entwined, aren't they?"

She places her hand in mine, and her eyes flutter open. "Yes."

I'm not sure if she means yes, she agrees with the sentiment, or yes, she agrees with what I want.

"Yes?"

When she smiles, her eyes light up, moon-kissed amethyst that enchants me to my soul. "Yes, Cain. I accept your terms. I'm yours."

PREVIEW

Atonement: A Dark Romance (Master's Protégé Book two)

CHAPTER ONE

Violet

"Keep your eyes straight ahead. Do not move away, even for a second."

Cain's deep rumble of a voice vibrates in my ear. Of *course* this is one of the very many ways he'd test me. Just hands me a gun that requires immense concentration to handle, gives me an instruction to keep my eyes on the target ahead, then hovers his magnificent, muscled body so close to mine I'm nearly trembling in anticipation.

"Bet no one else has target practice like *this*," I mutter, more than a little annoyed. I don't want to have target practice. I want to tear his clothes off and jump his bones, right now, right here, on the cold concrete floor of the target range. I'm annoyed I can't do that, and annoyed he's made me feel like a wanton slut.

"That's right, Violet," Cain says in my ear, as he ghosts his tongue over my ear lobe. I stifle a whimper. "There's no one else here who uses the target practice for the sole purpose of muffling their screams when they come."

"It's not the *sole* purpose," I mutter under my breath. I mean, I'm a damn good shot now.

I brace myself, grit my teeth, and pull the trigger. Fire explodes from the gun, the bullet tears into the paper target shaped like a human, and I watch with gleeful satisfaction as I tear a hole right between the eyes, the infamous "t box" shot. Lethal, every time.

"Well done, little protégé," Cain says with approval. Warmth flares across my chest at his praise. It's rare that he doles out praise to anyone, and sometimes I feel he's toughest on me. The others know I mean something to him, though we've kept our relationship under wraps, and he doesn't want anyone to think I get preferential treatment.

I do, though.

I *so* do.

"Tell me the three types of gunshots," he says, nestling his hands on my hips. He's been training me now for two months, and only a small portion of the training takes place with actual tactical work.

I try to stand up straighter, but his body's pressed up against mine. Not that I'm complaining. I reload my gun as I spout off details. "The three main types of gunshot wounds include non penetrating, perforating, and penetrating. Non-penetrating wounds mean the bullet grazed skin without embedding, perforating wounds involve an entrance and exit site, and penetrating wounds have an entrance site with no exit."

"Very good. Which type of gunshot do we aim for, Violet?"

I answer like I'm under his command, because it tickles my fancy. "Whichever is the most expedient, sir."

Sometimes we shoot to warn. Sometimes we shoot to injure. Sometimes we shoot to kill.

I hold my position, vividly aware of his heartbeat against my back and his warmth that surrounds me like a heated blanket. He'd kick anyone's ass for target practice while so close to another, but I know it's partly how he likes to test me.

I aim for the target, and pull the trigger again.

Bam. Hit the kidney, an excellent debilitating and potentially fatal shot. The perfect one to incapacitate and cause pain without immediate death, if we're feeling like we need to have al little chat.

"Good girl. Excellent."

I don't react. I don't want anyone to see how I bask in the little rays of his praise. It's kind of pathetic.

"Aim for the left shoulder."

I pull the trigger and stifle a grin when the paper target of a shoulder tears open.

"Heart."

Another on-point hit.

"Right shoulder."

Boom.

I don't wait for further instruction, but aim a few more shots, the last one landing straight in the groin area.

"Fuck, my balls clenched at that."

"Your balls clenched because it's twenty degrees out here. Did you see what I made for you?"

I grin at him over my shoulder, and he quickly brushes his mouth against mine. I didn't expect that, but I don't stop him. I love the feel of his hot, sensual mouth on mine, the way my body melts against him and my heartbeat quickens.

"No, baby," he whispers with a smile. "What'd you make for me?"

"It's a heart, see?"

He looks over my shoulder. "Ah, so it is. You shot a heart shape in a human body. If that's not the most romantic fucking thing I've ever seen…"

I grin. "I knew you'd like it."

"Should I frame it?" he teases, as I clean up the little table at the range and carefully put the ammo and guns away.

"Of course. Put it away so I can regift it to you on Valentine's Day."

"You're so damn romantic."

"I try."

He takes the gun out of my hand, lays it down on the table, and reaches for me.

"This is why you love target practice."

I gasp when his fingers tangle in my hair, his grip firm but just exactly what I need. My mouth parts to release a whimper he quickly swallows. His tongue touches mine. My belly melts.

My hands find their way around his hard, muscled back, grasping for purchase as he takes the kiss deeper. Harder. I meet his tongue with mine, relishing the sound of his deep, male groan.

"Tell me again," he grates in my ear, a firm command that makes my nipples hard. "The three types of gunshot wounds, Violet. Nice and slow."

"Non-penetrating," I say on a groan, as his fingers find the hem of my shirt and gently lift it. I feel the warmth of his touch on my belly, then one finger grazes the curve of my breast. He flickers a thumb over my bra-clad nipple. My body's used to his touch. My hips jerk.

He nods. I think I know what he's doing.

"Perforating." Strong fingers slide past the elastic of my leggings, past the silk top of my panties, and dive between my legs to do their magic. I open my legs and moan, surprised at how wet I am already. I shouldn't be. He knows how to play my body, how to work it to climax in any way he knows how.

"Good girl. And the last one?"

I close my eyes. "Penetrating."

Thick fingers plunge in my core, jerk upward, and I cry out from the sudden stabbing thrills that explode through me.

He's done wicked, dirty things to me in here, and it seems he's nowhere near finished.

"I fucking love to see you come," he growls in my ear, his hand cupped possessively around my pussy, still spasming. I breathe hard, then softer, slumping against him. I'm barely aware of where we are or what we're doing when he slides into one of the straight-backed chairs at the back of the range we keep for guests, and tugs me onto his lap.

It's been precisely six weeks and four days since we rescued his sister Skylar from a vindictive serial rapist. It feels much, much longer.

I've left my day job and moved into Cain's house in Salem, a large, rambling estate where many of his employees live. He treats them to the lap of luxury, as he should. They run a top secret, clandestine organization that charges top dollar. Their clients pay more for a job with Masters Enterprises than most people ever earn in their lifetime. Tonight's security detail, for example, runs a cool million dollars.

"Got a present for you, baby," Cain whispers in my ear.

"Cain—"

"You shouldn't buy me so many things," he finishes in a high-pitched voice. "Stop spoiling me. I don't need all these things."

I mutter under my breath. But when he nestles a heavy, large, solid black box onto my lap, I close my mouth. My heart beats a little faster.

"What's that?" I whisper.

"Open it and see."

My hand shakes when I slide my finger along the edge of the box top and gently lift it. I lean myself against his large, sturdy frame to help still the trembling, but it doesn't work. I'm shaking. I don't handle expensive gifts well, and something tells me this one's not cheap.

I don't deserve it, I think to myself, *whatever it is.*

He wouldn't like if he heard me saying that.

"It's way too big of a box for jewelry and way too small for a car."

His low, manly chuckle makes me smile.

"You don't want a car, baby. Even I know that. You want a truck."

Not just any truck, I want the gorgeous Toyota Tundra 4WD with the Rockstar Rims that sits in his driveway. The gorgeous force of nature with thirty-eight-inch mud terrain tires and black rawhide leather interior with blood-red inlay. *Swoon.*

I lift the lid, and my jaw drops open. I can't breathe for long seconds, my eyes water with tears, and my nose tingles. There's a lump lodged into my throat. I don't trust myself to speak.

"You deserve it, baby," he whispers in my ear. No. No one deserves a masterpiece like this, and most definitely not me.

"Is this the Wilson?" I whisper.

We were looking at high-end handguns the other day, and when my eyes fell on the Wilson Combat Tactical Supergrade, I almost lost my mind. It's absolutely *gorgeous,* handcrafted from carbon steel, the premier in defensive handguns.

Gunmetal gray with silver details, it's solidly built yet somehow lightweight. The handle's decorated in a pattern that looks like sunbursts. Every detail is finely crafted perfection.

"I had this custom made for you, baby." Of course he did. Cain Master doesn't do cookie cutter. "Takes eight rounds. Four-inch trigger pull, starburst grips, five inch carbon steel slide." He goes on about the details, front sight something something, blah blah

blah. I've got guns that I absolutely love. Some that have become like friends to me, comfortable in my palm and ready to shoot. But this… this was custom made for me.

"It's lightweight, beautiful, and deadly," he says.

"You do say the most romantic things."

I feel his stubble across my cheek when he kisses me, and while a thrill shimmers through my body, I'm focused on the stunning weapon I hold in my hand.

"I can't take this, Cain." I shake my head. It cost *five thousand dollars.*

"You can. You're worth it."

I shake my head, but he gently pushes me off his lap. "Go show me, Violet. Show me what you've got. We've got the security detail tonight, and if you're comfortable with it, you'll take this with you."

He's got harnesses and holsters galore for me to choose from, so that shouldn't be a problem.

I stand, new energy coursing through me with my new toy in hand. I tremble in anticipation as I slide the ammo into place. I've used his guns. I've borrowed guns.

I've never owned one.

I take in a deep breath, get into position, and aim.

Boom.

Boom.

Boom.

My God, it shoots as if enhanced with magic. Each bullet hits its mark with perfect precision.

This is it. I'm holding the weapon I'll use when I kill my parents' murderer.

Due to release October 22nd, 2021.

ABOUT THE AUTHOR

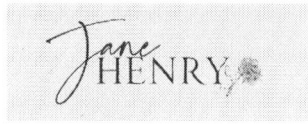

USA Today bestselling author Jane Henry pens stern but loving alpha heroes, feisty heroines, and emotion-driven happily-ever-afters. She writes what she loves to read: kink with a tender touch. Jane is a hopeless romantic who lives on the East Coast with a houseful of children and her very own Prince Charming.

You can find Jane here!

The Club (Jane Henry's fan page)

Website

Printed in Great Britain
by Amazon